"Sarah was my secretary, I admit. But we did not have an affair."

Tina folded her arms and practically rolled her eyes at him. "Oh, come now, Mr. Hunter, I didn't come down in the last shower. I know exactly what happened between you and Sarah. How you can stand there and deny having slept with her is beyond me."

"I am not the father of that baby, or any other baby. Honey, you've got the wrong man."

Tina actually smiled at him, an icy smile that set his teeth on edge. "You are Dominic Hunter, the head of Hunter & Associates, aren't you?"

"You know I am."

"Then I've got the right man. But if you insist on a DNA test, I won't object...."

He's a man of cool sophistication.
He's got pride, power and wealth.
At the top of his corporate ladder, he's a
ruthless businessman.
An expert lover—he's one hundred
percent committed to staying single.
His life runs like a well-oiled machine....

Until now. Because suddenly he's
responsible for a BABY!

His Baby.
An exciting new miniseries from
Harlequin Presents®
He's sexy, successful...
and he's facing up to fatherhood!

In April, look out for another His Baby title:
The Unexpected Wedding Gift
by Catherine Spencer
Harlequin Presents® #2101

MIRANDA LEE

Facing up to Fatherhood

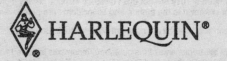

TORONTO • NEW YORK • LONDON
AMSTERDAM • PARIS • SYDNEY • HAMBURG
STOCKHOLM • ATHENS • TOKYO • MILAN • MADRID
PRAGUE • WARSAW • BUDAPEST • AUCKLAND

ISBN 0-373-12087-7

FACING UP TO FATHERHOOD

First North American Publication 2000.

Visit us at www.romance.net

Printed in U.S.A.

CHAPTER ONE

TINA glanced up at the towering office block, then down at the pram, and the baby lying within.

'Here we are, darling!' she announced to the pretty pink-clad infant. 'Your daddy's workplace. Unfortunately, your daddy'll be in a meeting all afternoon, according to his secretary. Didn't have time for any appointments. Which is just too bad, isn't it? Because he's going to see us today whether he likes it or not!'

Arching a well-plucked eyebrow, she angled the pram determinedly towards the revolving glass doors, hoping for more success than her encounter with the train doors earlier on. Manoeuvring a pram, Tina had found, was as hazardous as one of those wayward shopping trolleys, the kind whose wheels had a mind of their own. Still, she'd only been doing it for a week, so she supposed there were excuses for her ineptitude.

It was a struggle, but she finally emerged unscathed into the cavernous semicircular foyer with its acre or two of black granite flooring. Tina negotiated this pram-friendly surface with thankful ease, bypassing the busy reception desk and skirting several large lumps of marble masquerading as art, finally halting beneath the huge directory which hung on the wall beside the bank of lifts.

Hunter & Associates, she swiftly noted, occupied floors nineteen and twenty. Tina also noted Hunter & Associates carried no description of what services or utilities the company provided, other than to say 'Management' was on the twentieth floor.

This might have been a modest oversight, but Tina rather imagined it reflected its owner's character. Dominic Hunter arrogantly assumed everyone knew his company was one of Sydney's most successful stockbroking and investment firms.

He had also arrogantly assumed his affair with his secretary last year would never rise up to bite him on his arrogant backside.

But he was wrong!

Sarah might have been a softie. And a push-over where men were concerned. But Tina was not!

Sarah's daughter deserved the very best. And Tina aimed to make sure she got it. She would give Dominic Hunter a second chance to be a proper father to his beautiful little daughter. If he didn't come to the party willingly, then he would be made to pay. And pay handsomely. In this day of DNA testing, simply denying fatherhood was a thing of the past.

'Just let him try it, darling,' she informed the baby girl as she wheeled the pram into the lift. 'If he does, we're going to have his guts for garters!'

CHAPTER TWO

DOMINIC raised his eyes to the ceiling as he hung up the phone.

'Women!' he muttered frustratedly, before standing up to gather his papers together for that afternoon's meeting, almost knocking over a cold, half-drunk cup of coffee in the process. Only a desperate lunge and grab prevented coffee spilling all over his desk.

He righted the mug and plonked it well to one side, his sigh carrying total exasperation. He was having a really bad day.

His colleagues might have thought it was the present economic crisis which was causing his tetchy mood. But that wasn't the case. Dominic thrived on the challenges the financial arena kept throwing at him, finding great excitement and personal satisfaction in making money, both for himself and all his clients. He'd been called a stockmarket junkie more than once, and had to admit it was true.

No, Dominic could always cope with business problems. It was the opposite sex which was irritating the death out of him.

Frankly, he just didn't understand the species, especially their obsession with marriage and babies. Couldn't they see that, in this present day and age, the world would actually be better off with less of both? There certainly wouldn't be as many divorces, or so many unhappy neglected children!

But, no! Such common sense views never seemed

to cut the mustard with women. They went on wanting marriage and babies as though they were the pan-
acea for all the world's ills, instead of adding to them.

The same thing applied to romantic love. Crazy,
really. When had this unfortunate state ever brought
women—or men for that matter—any happiness?

Dominic had grown up in a household where that
kind of love had caused nothing but emotional torment and misery.

He wanted none of it. Love *or* marriage *or* babies—a fact reinforced in his early twenties when a
girlfriend had tried to trap him into marriage with a
false pregnancy.

The thought of imminent fatherhood and marriage
had horrified him. Perhaps his panic had had something to do with own father being a lousy parent—as
well as a faithless husband—producing a subcon-
scious fear he might turn out to be just as big a jerk
in that department. He'd already *looked* like the man.

Whatever, Dominic's relief at discovering the pregnancy had been a lie had been very telling. It had also
been his first intimate experience at just how far a
female would go in pursuit of that old romantic fantasy called 'love and marriage'.

After that sobering experience, Dominic always
took care of protection personally when having sex.
He was never swayed by any female's assertion that
she was on the pill, or that it was a 'safe' time of the
month. He also always made his position quite clear
to every woman he became involved with. Marriage
was not on his agenda, no matter what!

His mother found his views on the subject totally
unfathomable. With typical female logic, she simply
dismissed them as a temporary aberration.

'You'll change your mind one day,' she would say every now and then. 'When you fall in love...'

Now *that* was another romantic illusion his mother harboured. His *falling in love*! He'd never fallen in love in his life. And he had no intention of doing so. The very word 'falling' suggested a lack—and a loss—of control which he found quite distasteful, and which could only lead to one disastrous decision after another!

Fortunately for him, his mother had been able to channel her grandmotherly hopes up till now towards his younger brother, Mark, who'd married a couple of years back. Dominic had simply assumed Mark and his wife would reproduce in time, thereby letting him permanently off the hook.

But a few months ago his one and only sibling had unexpectedly arrived home and announced he was leaving his wife to go off to Tibet to become a Buddhist monk! To prove it, he'd promptly given all his considerable worldly goods to his rapidly recovering wife and taken off, his subsequent letters revealing he was happy as a lark living on some mountain-top monastery with only a yak for companionship!

It didn't take a genius to conclude there would be no imminent hope of a grandchild from *that* quarter!

Which had brought his widowed mother's focus right back on him, her only other offspring, and now her only other hope of providing her with a grandchild!

She'd been driving him mad with her none too subtle pressure, inviting all sorts of unattached females home to dinner. All of them beautiful. All of them sexy. And all of them wanting—or pretending to want—the same thing his mother wanted. Marriage and babies.

She'd just rung to check that he wouldn't be too late home for dinner tonight, because she'd invited Joanna Parsons over.

'The poor darling has been so lonely since Damien died,' Ida had purred down the line.

Lonely? Joanna Parsons? Dear God! The woman was a sexual vampire. Even before Damien's death, in a car crash six months ago, she'd done her best to seduce him. As a merry widow, there would be no holds barred!

Dominic liked his sex, but he liked it unencumbered, thank you very much. And with women who held the same views as he did. His current lady-friend was an advertising account executive whose marriage had broken up because she'd been already married to her job. Dominic saw her two or three times a week, either at her apartment after work or in a hotel room at lunchtimes, an arrangement which suited them both admirably.

Shani was thirty-two, an attractive brunette with a trim gym-honed body. She wasn't into endless fore-play or mindless chit-chat or sentimentality, the word 'love' never entering what little conversation they had. She was also fanatical when it came to her health. If ever Dominic might have been tempted to believe a woman when she said it was safe, it would have been Shani.

But long-ingrained habits died hard, and Dominic maintained a cynical distrust of the female psyche. It would never surprise him to discover that his latest bed-partner, no matter how career-minded, had fallen victim to her infernal biological clock. In his experience, not even the most unlikely female was immune to *that* disease!

Take the case of Melinda, his invaluable PA, who'd been with him for years and always said she wanted a career, not the role of wife and mother. So what happened? She'd turned thirty and in less than twelve months had married and left to have a baby. On top of that, she'd refused to come back to work, abandoning him totally for the home front.

He'd been most put out!

Naturally he'd had to take steps to ensure such a thing wasn't going to become a regular occurrence, though at the time finding a replacement for Melinda had been a right pain in the neck. There'd been no question of keeping the girl on who'd filled in during Melinda's supposedly temporary maternity leave. As efficient and sweet as Sarah was, beautiful, young, unattached females were out—a decision reinforced by what had happened when he'd taken Sarah out for a thank-you meal on the last evening of her employ.

Dominic shuddered to think that even *he* could become a temporary victim of his hormones, if the circumstances were right. He'd been between women at the time, and had drunk far too much wine with his meal. When he'd taken Sarah home in a taxi and walked her to the door of her flat she'd unexpectedly started to cry. Her louse of a boyfriend, it seemed, had just the day before dumped her for some other woman.

Dominic had only meant to comfort her, but somehow comfort had turned to something else and they'd ended up in bed together for the night. They'd both regretted it in the morning, both agreed not to mention it again.

Sarah had gone back to her normal job as a secretary in Accounts on the floor below his, and he'd met Shani at a dinner party that very weekend.

His new secretary, Doris, had started the following Monday morning.

Thank God for Doris.

Now Doris would never cause him any worries. She was fifty-four, for starters, happily married, with a healthy, undemanding husband and grown-up children who didn't live at home. She didn't mind working late when required, and didn't object to making him coffee at all hours of the day. If his tendency to untidiness bothered her—and he suspected it did—she didn't say so to his face, just quietly cleaned up after him. A woman of great common sense and tact was Doris.

The intercom on his desk buzzed and he flicked the switch. 'Yes, Doris?'

'The others are waiting for you in the boardroom, Mr Hunter.'

That was another thing he liked about Doris.

She called him Mr Hunter, and not Dominic. It had a nice, respectful ring about it, and made him feel older than his thirty-three years.

'Yes, yes, I'm coming. Hold all calls, will you, Doris? Absolutely no interruptions. We have a lot of work to get through this afternoon.'

The lift doors opened, and Tina steered the pram, along with the now sleeping infant, onto the twentieth floor. Straight ahead was a long glass wall with floor-to-ceiling glass doors upon which was written in gold lettering 'Hunter & Associates—Management'.

Beyond was another sea of black granite, dominated by a shiny black reception desk.

Tina wondered caustically if the glossy blonde perched behind the desk had been chosen personally by Dominic Hunter himself.

Maybe he had a penchant for blondes. She recalled Sarah saying something about the big boss being present at her second interview for Hunter & Associates, after which she'd swiftly been hired.

Of course Sarah hadn't just been any old blonde. Though her long fair hair had been her crowning glory, she'd been equally striking of face and figure. Her stunning looks had been a problem all her life, and hadn't brought her any happiness. Men hadn't been able to keep their eyes, or their hands, off.

Poor, sweet Sarah had always believed the declarations of love which had poured forth from her current pursuer's mouth. After she'd become a secretary working in the city, she'd been especially susceptible to the smoothly suited variety of male, especially good-looking ones with dark hair, bedroom blue eyes and a convincing line of patter to get her into the cot and keep her there without actually offering any solid commitment.

Sarah had been a sucker for that combination every time, always believing herself *in love*. Once *in love*, Sarah had become her latest lover's doormat, thinking that was the road to the wedding ring and the family of her own she'd always craved.

Naturally it had never turned out that way, and Sarah had been dumped in the end. It had driven Tina mad to watch her friend being used and abused by one silver-tongued creep after another. Married, divorced or single, it hadn't mattered. If they'd told Sarah they loved her, she'd been putty in their hands.

Tina had tried to give solace and advice after each break-up, but her patience had worn thin over the years. She'd finally seen red when, shortly after Sarah had been promoted to the plum job of PA to Dominic Hunter, Sarah had confessed to being *in love* again. When pressed, she'd admitted the object of her affections was her new boss. A terrible argument had ensued. Tina had told Sarah that she'd sleep with any man if he said he loved her, and Sarah had retaliated that Tina had a heart of stone, was incapable of really loving anything or anyone but herself.

They were the last words the two friends had said to each other. That had been just over a year ago.

And now Sarah was dead.

Tina's chin began to wobble. She had to swallow hard to stop herself from bursting into tears.

'I won't let you down, Sarah,' she whispered as she gazed down at Sarah's beautiful little baby girl. 'Your Bonnie's going to have everything you would have wanted for her. Every possible advantage. There will be no feeling of not being loved or wanted. No hand-me-down clothes. No leaving school at fifteen. As for Welfare and foster homes! Never! Not as long as I've got breath in my body!'

Hardening herself for the fray which undoubtedly lay ahead, Tina pushed the glass door open with the pram and forged over to the desk.

'I'm here to see Dominic Hunter,' she announced firmly to the glamorous green-eyed blonde. 'And, yes, before you ask, I do have an appointment,' came the bald lie.

Faint heart never won fat turkey, Tina always be-

lieved. She'd never have gained entry to the most
prestigious drama school in Australia if she hadn't
been confident of her acting ability. Admittedly, she'd
auditioned for three consecutive years before she'd
won one of the coveted positions of entry. But that
wasn't a measure of ability, she'd always told herself.
It was as hard to get into AIDA as Fort Knox!

The blonde directed her towards a long polished
corridor which led into another smaller reception area
covered in plush dark blue carpet. The pram wheels
immediately floundered in the thick pile, then came
to a rebellious halt.

'Can I help you?' came the puzzled but cool query.
Tina
glanced up at the severely suited woman seated behind the now familiar shiny black desk.

Dominic Hunter's secretary, Tina concluded with
much surprise. For the woman wasn't blonde. Or
pretty. Or young.

Tina wondered cynically if Dominic Hunter had
finally learned his lesson about mixing business and
pleasure.

'I'm here to see Dominic,' she returned, just as
coolly.

The secretary frowned. 'Mr Hunter is in a meeting
all afternoon. He specifically asked that I not disturb
him for anything.'

Tina finally got the wheels straight and bulldozed
the pram across the carpet. 'I doubt he meant me,'
she said, stopping in front of the desk. 'Or his daughter, here.'

The woman's eyes widened as she rose to peer over
her desk, down into the pram. 'His...daughter?' she
repeated, startled.

'That's right,' Tina answered crisply. 'Her name is Bonnie. She's three months old. Could you please tell Dominic that she's here and would like to meet her father at long last?'

The secretary blinked, then cleared her throat. 'Er…perhaps you'd best come into Mr Hunter's office and I'll go get him.'

Tina's smile was icy. 'What a good idea.'

Dominic Hunter's office was another surprise. Although the room was huge, the carpet still plush, and the view of Sydney breathtaking, it was an office laid out for working, not impressing. There were several work stations around the walls, each with its own computer, printer, phone, fax and swivel chair. Every computer was still on, winking figures at Tina. Every surface was messy, littered with papers of various kinds. The main desk wasn't much better.

The secretary made an exasperated sound at the sight of it, shaking her head as she lifted a half-drunk coffee mug from its glossy black surface, Snatching a tissue out of a nearby box, she vigorously rubbed at the stain left behind, muttering 'truly' under her breath.

Meanwhile, Tina lowered herself into one of the two empty upright chairs facing the main desk, crossing her long legs and angling the pram closer so she could check that Bonnie was still sleeping.

'What a good little baby you are,' she crooned softly as she tucked the pink bunny rug tightly around the tiny feet. When she'd finished, and looked up, it was to find the secretary staring at her as though she'd just landed from Mars.

'I dare say Mr Hunter will be with you shortly,'

the woman said, and, shaking her head again, left the room, shutting the door behind her.

That same door burst open less than two minutes later, and Tina's head whipped round to encounter her first view of Bonnie's father.

Dominic Hunter was even more of a surprise than his secretary, or his office.

Yes, he was tall, as she'd anticipated. And dark-haired. And handsome, in a hard-boned fashion. He even had blue eyes.

But, despite all that, the man glaring at her across the room didn't fit the picture she'd formed of him in her imagination.

Sarah's lovers had usually been suave and elegant, perfectly groomed and beautifully dressed. They'd oozed a smooth charm and sophisticated sex appeal which girls of Sarah's upbringing seemed to find irresistibly attractive.

Dominic Hunter hardly fitted that description.

He marched into the room, a menacingly macho male with his big, broad-shouldered body and close-cropped haircut. The sleeves of his blue shirt were rolled up as though ready for battle, his tie was missing, and the top button around his muscular neck undone. His scowl was such that his dark straight brows momentarily met above his nose.

Frankly, he looked more like a construction site foreman about to bawl out his labourers rather than a successful stockbroker who should have been able to handle even *this* sticky situation with some aplomb.

Grinding to a halt next to the pram, he glowered, first down at Bonnie and then up at Tina again. 'I hear you're claiming this is my daughter!' he snarled.

Tina refused to be intimidated by this macho bully.

She wondered what on earth Sarah had seen in the man. She could only speculate that he came up better in bed than out of it.

'That's right,' she said.

He gave her a look which would have sent poor Sarah running for cover. Tina began to understand why her friend hadn't approached Bonnie's biological father for help and support a second time. When this man finished with a woman, he would expect her to stay finished.

But she wasn't Sarah, was she?

Tina almost smiled as she thought of what Mr Hunter was up against this time. Brother, was he in for a surprise or two of his own!

'Wait here,' he growled.

'I'm certainly not going anywhere,' she said in a calm voice, and received another of those blistering looks.

Tina didn't even blink, holding his killer gaze without the slightest waver.

He stared hard at her for several more seconds, then whirled and left the room, slamming the door shut behind him.

Tina sat there, whistling and swinging her left foot. It was to be hoped Mr Macho was out there getting a grip on himself and finding some manners. Or at least some common sense. Because she wasn't about to go away, not this side of Armageddon!

The minutes ticked steadily away.

Five...

Ten...

Her blood pressure began to rise a little, but she'd been mentally ready for this. She hadn't expected the man to come to the party willingly, not when he'd already denied paternity, given Sarah money for a termination and sent her on her way.

Frankly, Tina had expected nothing from him, and he was living up to her low opinion of men of his ilk. Obviously she had a fight on her hands to get the financial support she needed to raise Sarah's daughter in the manner Bonnie deserved.

But she enjoyed a good fight, didn't she? She was always at her best when her back was against the wall.

The sound of the door finally opening had her swivelling in her chair with an aggressive glint in her eye. How dared he keep her waiting this long?

The sight of two burly security guards entering startled her, then sent her blood pressure sky-high. So *that* was how he was going to play it, was it?

Gritting her teeth, she stood up and gave the approaching guards a haughty look of disdain. 'I gather Mr Hunter won't be returning?'

'That's right, ma'am,' the bigger and older of the two informed her. 'He said to tell you that next time he'd be calling the police.'

'Really? Well, we'll see about that, won't we? No, that's not necessary!' she snapped when the guard who'd spoken forcibly took her by the elbow. 'I'll go quietly.'

Despite her protests, the two guards still escorted her till she was outside the building.

She stood there on the pavement for several moments, glaring up at the top floors, struggling to get her temper under control. She imagined the bastard peering back down at her from his lofty position, smug and smirking with triumph.

'You'll get yours, Dominic Hunter,' she threatened

under her breath. 'I'm going to take you to the cleaners!'

Scooping in several deep breaths, Tina forcibly slowed her pounding heart and found some much-needed composure. Her brain finally began ticking over, and she started wondering *why* Bonnie's father was so sure of his ground that he would dare have her thrown out. It was a stupid move to bluff about paternity in this day and age.

No matter what else he might be, Dominic Hunter was not stupid.

It suddenly dawned on Tina that he probably believed Sarah had had that termination he'd paid for, which meant he might not have realised Bonnie was the baby Sarah had come to see him about, despite her being the right age. He possibly thought Bonnie was another baby entirely, and she, Tina, was the mother. When he'd stared so hard at her it could have been because he was trying to recall if he'd ever slept with her or not. Since he hadn't, naturally he'd assumed she was trying to pull off some kind of false paternity suit.

That had to be it!

Tina could have kicked herself. She should have said straight up that she wasn't the biological mother.

'Your new mummy's an idiot,' she told the now wide-awake infant as she wheeled the pram towards the taxi rank on the corner. 'But don't worry, I have a contingency plan. Since I've temporarily blotted my copybook with your father, we'll go see your grandmother and gain entry that way. Yes, I know you're getting hungry and wet. I'll feed and change you in the taxi. I've brought everything with me. Bottles. Nappies. Spare clothes. Aren't you impressed?'

Several passersby glanced over their shoulders at the tall, striking brunette wheeling the brand-new navy pram along the pavement, oblivious of everything but the baby to whom she was talking fifteen to the dozen.

'Just wait till your nanna sees how beautiful you are. And how good. She won't be able to resist you. I couldn't, could I? And look at me? A hard-nosed piece if ever there was one. Or so your real mummy used to say. And she was probably right. But she wasn't right about my not being able to love anything or anybody. No, my darling, she was quite wrong about that...'

CHAPTER THREE

THE nerve of the woman! The darned nerve!

Dominic fumed as he glared down at the pavement below and watched her pushing the pram down the street. What on earth did she think she was playing at? How did she think she was going to get away with such an outrageous claim? Even if he was one of the unlucky few whose condom had failed, did she honestly imagine that he wouldn't remember sleeping with someone like her?

She wasn't the sort of female he would forget in a hurry. For one thing, she was exactly his type. Dominic had always been attracted to tall, slim brunettes with interesting faces and dark, glittering eyes who made it obvious from their first meeting that men were not their favourite species. He liked the challenge of getting them into bed, then watching them abandon their feminist aggression for the short time his sexual know-how—and their own basic needs—overcame their natural antagonism. He'd had several rather lengthy involvements with such women, and prided himself on keeping them as friends afterwards.

Oh, yes, he would have remembered having sex with…damn it all, he didn't even know her name! She'd only supplied Doris with the name of her baby.

Bonnie.

As if that would mean anything to him!

He watched till she disappeared under a street awning, certain that that would be the last he'd see of her.

Perversely, he almost regretted having had her thrown out so hastily. He should have questioned her further, listened to her tall tale, found out what it was she wanted from him.

Money, he supposed, as he turned from the window and strode across his office towards the door. What else could she possibly have wanted?

He ground to a halt with his hand reaching for the doorknob, his forehead creasing into a frown.

But why had *he* been the target of her attempted con? It wasn't as though he had a reputation for indiscriminate and promiscuous behaviour. He certainly wasn't the sort of man who could be convinced he'd slept with some stranger whilst drunk or under the influence of drugs. He never drank to *that* much excess and he never took drugs!

Maybe she'd mixed him up with someone else, he speculated. Maybe *she* was the one who'd forgotten who it was she'd slept with. Maybe the father of her baby was someone else working at Hunter & Associates. Or a stockbroker from another firm. Someone who looked like him, perhaps.

Yes, that had to be it, he decided firmly. It was a case of mistaken identity.

Now, forget her and get back to work, he ordered himself. You've wasted enough time for one day!

Mrs Hunter's address was in Clifton Gardens, an old but exclusive Northshore suburb which hugged Sydney Harbour and where even the simplest house had an asking price of a million.

Mrs Hunter's house, however, wasn't simple. It turned out to be a stately sandstone residence, two-storeyed, with a wide wooden verandah. The block was huge, and the gardens, a visual delight, immaculately kept.

Tina frowned at the sight, and the conclusions such a property evoked. Dominic Hunter's family possessed old money, the kind which inevitably produced people who thought they were a cut above ordinary folk. Arrogance was as natural to them as breathing.

If Mrs Hunter proved to be such a snob, maybe she wouldn't welcome an illegitimate grandchild into her life, regardless of how adorable Bonnie was. Maybe she would be as sceptical—and as rude—as her son. Maybe she would swiftly show Tina and Bonnie the door, as he had done.

Tina's resolve wavered only momentarily, her confidence regained by a glance at the beautiful baby in her arms.

No woman in the world could resist Bonnie, she reasoned. Not if she had any kind of heart at all!

Tina was climbing out of the taxi before a second dampening thought occurred to her. What if Dominic Hunter's mother wasn't at home?

She'd set about discovering the woman's existence and her address that morning, *after* she'd been told by Dominic Hunter's secretary that she couldn't see the great man himself that day.

Severely irritated at the time, Tina had swiftly rung Dominic Hunter's secretary back, putting on an English accent and pretending to be an embarrassed florist who was supposed to deliver flowers to Mr Hunter's mother that day but had lost her particulars.

At the time, she hadn't even known if his mother was still of this world. Presuming he did *have* a mother. It would never surprise Tina to find out that the Dominic Hunters of this world were spawned in a test-tube. Or cloned from some other selfish macho creep with a megalomania complex.

A couple of minutes later she had hung up, with everything she needed to know. Mrs Hunter *was* still alive and well. And Tina knew where she lived.

She'd been going to go straight to the grandmother, but an indignant anger had sent her to Bonnie's father first. An impulsive decision.

Turning up on Mrs Hunter's doorstep without even ringing first wasn't much better.

Tina sighed. 'Would you mind waiting a few moments till I check to see if anyone's at home?' she asked the taxi driver as he paid him. 'I just realised the lady of the house might be out.'

'No sweat,' the driver said, and walked over to open the front gate for her.

Giving him an appreciative smile, Tina popped Bonnie back in the pram and set off up the paved front path, feeling too nervous now to admire the bloom-filled rose-beds which dotted the spacious front yard. It had been one thing to confront Bonnie's father. She'd known he was going to be difficult from the start.

His mother was proving a different kettle of fish entirely.

Although Tina tried to feel confident of the woman's reaction, she really could only hope.

But, oh, how she hoped! She desperately wanted Bonnie to have a grandmother who would lavish love upon her in the way only a grandmother could.

Not that Tina had any personal experience of a grandmother's love. But she gathered they specialised in the sort of unconditional affection and outrageous spoiling which both she and Sarah had only dreamt about during their growing-up years.

She also wanted Mrs Hunter to talk her son into recognising his daughter and agreeing to help support Bonnie financially, *without* Tina having to resort to legal pressures.

Pulling the pram to a halt at the base of the four stone steps which led up onto the wide wooden ve-randah, Tina put on the brake, then left the pram there while she hurried up the steps and rang the front door-bell.

For a nerve-racking twenty seconds, it looked as if no one was home, but then the door opened and there stood a woman of about sixty. Casually dressed in navy slacks and a floral blouse, she was tall and slim, with a handsome face and short, naturally grey hair. Best of all, there was a reassuring softness in her in-telligent blue eyes.

'Yes?' she said with an enquiring smile.

'Are you Mrs Hunter?' Tina asked.

'Yes, I am, dear. How can I help you?'

The dear did it. And the sweet offer of help. Tina had studied human psychology during the course of her acting career, and had become a pretty good judge in assessing character, especially when it came to women.

Mrs Hunter was no snob, for starters. Most impor-tant of all, she was kind.

Smiling with relief, Tina turned and waved to the taxi driver. 'It's okay,' she called. 'You can go now.'

'Righto.'

She turned back, just as the woman spotted the pram at the bottom of the steps. It was facing the house so that she could see Bonnie's sweet little face quite clearly.

'Oh, what a beautiful-looking baby!' she exclaimed, and moved down the steps for a closer look. 'A girl, I presume?' she said, glancing up at Tina over her shoulder.

'Yes.'

'May I hold her? She's wide awake.'

'Please do.'

A warm, squishy feeling settled in Tina's stomach as she watched the woman carefully scoop her grandchild up and start rocking her. Even after the seven short days Tina had cared for Bonnie she knew nothing enchanted the child more than being held and rocked in just that way. She would never cry while someone was doing that. She would just lie there and gaze up at the person rocking her, a look of total bliss on her lovely little face.

'What's her name?' her unwitting grandmother asked.

'Bonnie.'

'And yours, dear?'

'Tina. Tina Highsmith.'

'So, what are you selling, Tina?' Mrs Hunter asked while she smiled down at Bonnie. 'If you're an Avon lady, then I'm sorry, but I don't wear make-up any more other than a bit of lipstick. If you're with that other mob, then I also already have everything that opens and shuts in the houseware department. My son has no imagination when it comes to presents and always gives me something for the house. He's into practicality, is Dominic,' she added ruefully.

'Actually, Mrs Hunter, I'm not selling anything.

And it's your son, Dominic, I've come to see you about.'

This got her attention, startled blue eyes blinking up to stare at Tina. 'Dominic? Really? What about?'

'About Bonnie, there,' she said, nodding towards the baby. Tina swallowed, steeling herself for any possible negative reaction to her next announcement. She could only hope the woman was as nice as she seemed. 'She…she's Dominic's daughter.'

Tina was amazed at the speed and intensity of the various emotions which raced across Mrs Hunter's face. Shock gave way to a moment's uninhibited joy, swiftly followed by a deeply troubled concern.

She walked slowly up the steps to stand close to Tina, her expression still troubled. 'Does Dominic know?' she asked warily.

'I tried to tell him today, but I made a stupid mistake in the telling and he had Security throw me out of the building.'

Concern gave way to outrage. 'He *what*?'

'It was my fault, Mrs Hunter,' Tina explained hurriedly. 'I see that now. When I told him that Bonnie was his daughter I forgot to add that I am *not* the mother. I think he took one look at me, knew I was a stranger to him, and jumped to the conclusion I was trying to operate some kind of scam.'

Outrage changed to puzzlement. 'If you're not the mother…then, who is? Your sister?'

'No. My best friend.' Tina swallowed as that awful lump filled her throat, the one which always came when she thought of Sarah's dying. 'Sarah worked at Hunter & Associates all last year. She was Dominic's secretary from late July till the 25th November. Bonnie was born on August 19th. Sarah was critically injured when she was knocked down by a bus last month. She...she lived a few days, but didn't make it. Before she died, she made me Bonnie's legal guardian. Her birth certificate actually says 'father unknown', but I know Bonnie's father is your son.'

'You're sure?'

'*Very* sure, Mrs Hunter.'

Mrs Hunter was frowning. 'Did your friend actually tell you Dominic was the father of her baby?'

Tina hesitated. She didn't want to lie to the woman. It was just that the truth was so complicated, and possibly confusing to anyone who hadn't known Sarah well. The actual evidence Tina had concerning the identity of Bonnie's father was largely circumstantial, and partly second-hand. Mrs Hunter might think Tina was jumping to conclusions, but she knew better.

'Sarah and I told each other everything,' she said firmly at last, happy that this had been the truth—at least till they'd parted company. 'We were more like sisters than friends. Your son is Bonnie's father all right, Mrs Hunter. A DNA test should remove any doubt, however, if he continues to deny paternity.'

'What...what do you mean...*continues*?'

'Sarah went to see him when she found out she was pregnant. Dominic refused to believe the baby was his, though he did give her some money for a termination.'

'Which she obviously didn't have...'

'No. Sarah didn't believe in abortion.'

'Thank God,' the woman sighed, and smiled down at the baby in her arms before glancing up at Tina, tears in her eyes. 'I've always wanted a grandchild. You've no idea. I honestly thought I would never have one. Dominic was so adamant about not wanting marriage and children. And then his brother, Mark...well—'

She broke off and frowned at Tina. 'You said you were made the baby's legal guardian. Why is that, Tina? I know you said you were like a sister to this Sarah, but what about the child's maternal grandparents? Or aunts and uncles?'

'Sarah's mother died in a house fire when she was nine. Sarah never knew her father, or her grandparents. Her mum was a bit of a black sheep, you see. Ran away from her home in the country to the city when she was a teenager. She wasn't married when she had Sarah. I gather the father abandoned them before she was born. So, no, there are no close relatives interested in Bonnie. I'm all she's got at the moment.'

'I see. And what is *your* situation, dear? Are you married?'

'No, I'm not.'

Mrs Hunter's expression was thoughtful. 'I see. Er...are going to raise little Bonnie all by yourself, then?'

'I will if I have to, Mrs Hunter. But I'd prefer to have some help. I haven't any family, either, you see. My mother died in the same house fire Sarah's did. She was an unmarried mother too, you see. And a runaway as well.'

Not to mention a woman of the night. *Both* women had been. But Tina thought it best not to bring up too much of their unsavoury backgrounds lest Mrs Hunter be the sort of person who thought such things were hereditary and not environmental.

'When Welfare could find no relatives who wanted us,' she went on matter-of-factly, 'Sarah and I spent

the rest of our growing-up years in a state institution.'
When they hadn't been fostered out to people, that
was.

'Goodness. You poor things!'

'We survived, Mrs Hunter. But you can understand
how we became so close. Sarah has entrusted me with
the care and upbringing of her daughter and I aim to
make sure she has the very best. I have no intention
of Bonnie ever ending up like we did, with no money,
and no adult to love and care for her.'

'You won't have to worry about that, dear. I'll be
here for her, and for you. And so will Dominic, once
I have a word or two with him. You can depend on
that! Look, I think you'd best come inside and tell
me absolutely everything. Then I think you'd best
stay till Dominic gets home this evening and we can
have a family pow-wow over all this.'

Tina was taken aback. 'Your son lives with you?'

'Well, yes...he does.'

'Oh, dear!'

'He's not a Mummy's boy, if that's what you're
thinking. His decision to live with me was a practical
decision, not a sentimental one.'

'Believe me,' Tina said drily, 'I don't think your
son is a Mummy's boy. It's just that he's not going
to be pleased to find me here when he comes home.
Maybe you could ring him at the office and forewarn
him.'

'Absolutely not! No! He doesn't deserve forewarn-
ing,' she said brusquely. 'Besides, Fridays are never
a good day to ring Dominic at the office. I've already
rung him once today and received a very poor reception. Which reminds me. I'd best ring Joanna and
cancel her dinner invitation for tonight.'

'Not because of me, I hope,' Tina said, while wondering who Joanna was. A friend of Mrs Hunter's? Or Dominic's?

Mrs Hunter smiled a strange little smile. 'Not at all, dear. She's just a widow friend of mine. She can come another night. I'm a widow too, so little Bonnie won't be having a grandfather, I'm afraid. But you'll have me, won't you, darling?' she crooned down at the baby. 'Now, come along, dear, you bring the pram and I'll carry Bonnie. We'll have a cup of tea and a nice long chat. Then, afterwards, we might fill in the rest of the afternoon down at the shopping mall, buying a few little things for Bonnie here. Would you mind?'

'Oh, er...not at all.'

Off the woman went, making baby talk at Bonnie as she went, leaving Tina to do as ordered, trailing after her with the pram in rather a daze. There she'd been, thinking Mrs Hunter was such a sweet, gentle soul.

Which she *was*. But she was also a whirlwind of energy and decisiveness. Tina supposed it was unlikely that a too soft or susceptible personality could have produced a son like Dominic Hunter.

Dominic Hunter...

A lesser girl might have quailed to think of his reaction when he first spied her in his home this evening. She could just imagine it. Those hard blue eyes of his would narrow dangerously. The thick straight brows above them would beetle together again while smoke would waft from his flared nostrils. His broad shoulders would broaden while that huge chest of his would fill with outraged air. He would be ready to explode in seconds!

Tina smiled to herself.

She could hardly wait.

CHAPTER FOUR

DOMINIC considered being deliberately late home. He even contemplated ringing his mother at the last moment and claiming a fictitious business dinner in town.

But cowardice wasn't really his bag and he climbed into his blue BMW just before six and headed for the bridge. He would endure the dinner but had no intention of making any effort with that woman.

With a bit of luck Damien's merry widow—and his matchmaking mother—would finally see he was a lost cause where she was concerned. Lord, nothing turned him off quicker than gold-digging females who gushed all over him.

Blondes weren't really his thing, either. Nor double D cup breasts which jiggled like unset bowls of jelly.

Give him a tall, slender brunette, with long legs, a tight butt and firm boobs, and he was instantly interested. Make her a challenge and the combination was irresistible.

Joanna Parsons was neither.

An image of the brunette who'd been in his office today popped into his mind.

Again.

She'd been doing that all afternoon, even distracting him from work on several occasions.

Still, she'd been deliciously sexy in those tight white pedal-pusher pants and chest-hugging white ribbed top. Her hair was sexy too. Long and dark and kind of wild-looking, just like its owner.

Pity she was a con-artist. Or a fool.

Dominic was wondering which she might be when he turned into the driveway and parked the car outside the double garage. He still hadn't made up his mind by the time he slipped in the back door.

He was halfway up the stairs, heading for the sanctuary of his bedroom and private *en suite* bathroom when the sound of a baby crying stopped him in his tracks.

Frowning, Dominic turned and listened. It seemed to be coming from the front living room.

The television?

Not the television, he decided when the cries came again. Too loud. And too…real.

An appalling possibility popped into his mind.

Surely not, he thought. She wouldn't *dare*!

But then the baby cried again and he knew she had.

Whirling, he flew back down the stairs and over to the doorway of the room in question, disbelief and fury sending his blood pressure sky-high.

And there she was, large as life, wheeling a pram up and down on the polished wooden floor, singing very softly as she did so.

Dominic had opened his mouth to let her have it when she abruptly stopped the singing, and the wheeling. When she bent over to inspect the suddenly silent contents of the pram, the sight of those already tight white pants pulling even tighter across her extremely attractive derrière made him almost forget how angry he was for a moment.

But only for a moment.

'Hey, you there!' he boomed out.

She spun round, her dark hair flying out in a shining halo before settling more sedately on her slender shoulders. Her dark eyes flashed with extreme irritation as she hurried over, her fingers pressed to her lips.

'Hush up, for pity's sake,' she hissed. 'I've had the devil of a time getting her off to sleep. I think it's the strange house. Normally she goes off like clockwork after her bottle.'

Before he could say another word, she put a firm hand on his chest and pushed him backwards into the hallway, after which she carefully closed the door behind them, as though this whole scenario was perfectly normal and reasonable.

Dominic could only shake his head in amazement. Not a con-woman, he decided in total exasperation. A fool! A deliciously attractive fool, but a fool nevertheless!

'I don't know what you've told my mother,' he muttered, 'but you've got the wrong man. I am *not* the father of your baby.'

'Keep your shirt on, Mr Hunter. I never said you were.'

Instant bewilderment scrambled his brains. 'Huh?' was all he could manage.

'You can't be the father of *my* baby because I don't have one,' she explained, as though he were an idiot. 'I should have told you in your office but I simply didn't think. Bonnie belongs to Sarah.'

'Sarah?' he repeated blankly.

The brunette gave him a very droll look. 'I hope you're not going to tell me you don't know Sarah, either. Sarah Palmer,' she repeated coldly. 'In case you've forgotten, she was your secretary for several months last year, Mr Hunter, during which time you had an affair with her.'

Shock held Dominic speechless for a split second. But then anger swept back in. If Sarah thought she was going to pin the paternity of a baby on him on the strength of that one night, then she could think again!

'Sarah was my secretary, I admit,' he ground out. 'But we did *not* have an affair!'

The brunette folded her arms and practically rolled her eyes at him. 'Oh, come now, Mr Hunter. I didn't come down in the last shower. I know exactly what happened between you and Sarah. How you can stand there and deny having slept with her is beyond me!'

'I don't deny having slept with her,' he bit out. 'But it was only the once and I used protection. I repeat, I am not the father of that baby, or any other baby. As I said to you before, honey, you've got the wrong man.'

She actually smiled at him, an icy smile which set his teeth on edge. 'You are Dominic Hunter, the head of Hunter & Associates, aren't you?'

'You know damned well I am.'

'Then I've got the right man. But if you insist on a DNA test, I won't object.'

'A DNA test!' he exploded. 'I'm not having any damned DNA test!'

'Oh, yes, you are, Dominic.'

Dominic spun round to find his mother eyeing him with one of those stern looks which spelt her complete unwillingness to be persuaded otherwise. He knew because he'd seen that look many times during his lifetime. He groaned, then sighed his resignation to the inevitable. If he didn't succumb to a DNA test his life was going to be hell!

Still, once he'd calmed down a little, Dominic realised it was probably a good idea to have the test done. What better way to back his denial of paternity than with irretrievable scientific proof?

'Very well,' he agreed, with a return to composure, and both women looked surprised, even the dark-eyed brunette.

Who in hell *was* she? he began wondering. And what was she to Sarah? Her sister, perhaps?

He stared at her, thinking she looked nothing like Sarah at all. 'So tell me, Miss Know-it-all, why didn't Sarah come and see me in person about this baby of hers? Why send someone else in her place? Don't tell me it's because she's afraid of me because I won't believe that.'

Dominic was taken aback when those coal-black eyes, which till now had held such cynicism and contempt for him, suddenly shimmered with tears. When his mother walked over and put a comforting arm around the girl's shoulders, the penny dropped.

Sarah was dead.

That beautiful, sweet, lovely girl was dead.

His heart squeezed tight, and he wondered how she'd died. In childbirth, perhaps? But surely that kind of thing didn't happen these days.

'Sarah was killed in a road accident a couple of weeks ago,' his mother explained before he could ask, her own eyes reproachful towards him. 'She stepped out in front of a bus and was critically injured. Witnesses said she seemed to be daydreaming. Sarah didn't have any close relatives so she made Tina

Bonnie's legal guardian. They were best friends. Tina's come here today to see if we'll help raise the child.'

'That's all very sad,' Dominic said. 'And I'd be glad to give Tina some money, if that will help out. But, Mum, I am *not* Sarah's baby's father.'

His mother nodded. 'I appreciate you probably believe that, son. It explains your otherwise appalling behaviour. But Tina says Sarah told her you were the father for certain. She also said Sarah came to you and told you about her pregnancy when she was just a few weeks along. You denied you were the father back then, but gave her some money for a termination.'

'But that's just not true!' Dominic denied, truly shocked. 'If Sarah told you this, then she lied,' he directed forcibly at the brunette, who seemed to have swiftly recovered from the threat of tears to look at him coldly once more, her mouth pursed with scorn. 'I swear to you, I knew nothing of Sarah's pregnancy. Neither did she come and see me about it.'

The brunette's already disapproving lips curled over in even more derision. 'Sarah didn't tell lies.'

'Oh, for pity's sake, everyone tells lies!' he snapped.

'Do they indeed?'

Her sarcasm stung, as did her ongoing scepticism. She didn't believe a word he'd said. Dominic wasn't used to having his credibility doubted, and he didn't like it one bit.

He glared into those hard black eyes of hers, but they held his easily, and scornfully. Suddenly, he was overwhelmed by the most amazingly strong feeling, a mad compulsion to *make* her believe him, to take her in his arms and kiss that contemptuous mouth of

hers till she melted against him, till she was all soft
and compliant, till she was incapable of disbelieving,
or denying him anything.

His head whirled with the dark intensity of his desires, his hands actually twitching with the urge to
grab her right then and there. If his mother hadn't
been standing guard he might actually have done so.

The realisation stunned him. For he wasn't that
kind of man. Not normally.

Shaken at such an uncharacteristic loss of control,
he curled his wayward fingers into fists and jammed
them into his trouser pockets, only to discover to his
horror that he was partially aroused.

He could not believe it. Never in his life had a
woman got under his skin like this. He was torn between a black fury and an even blacker frustration.
The more he tried to will his flesh into subsidence,
the harder it became. Finally, he whipped his hands
out of his pockets and did up the buttons on his suit
jacket, at the same time drawing himself up tall in an
outer display of dignity.

The irony of his actions was not lost on him, but
be damned if he was going to risk being humiliated
in front of this female.

'You actually believe all this rubbish?' he demanded of his mother, looking for distraction in argument.

'Tina showed me a photograph of Sarah,' she replied coolly. 'She's one of the most beautiful girls
I've ever seen.'

'Meaning I wouldn't have been able to resist her,
is that it?'

'Most men couldn't, Mr Hunter,' the object of his
torment piped up. 'Especially when Sarah imagined

herself in love with them. She confessed to me she was in love with you last October, not long before Bonnie must have been conceived. When Sarah was in love with a man, there wasn't anything she wouldn't do for them.'

Not like you, Dominic thought as he glared at her scorn-filled face. You would never be any man's slave.

Which only made him want her all the more.

The discovery of where this over-the-top and stunningly uncontrollable desire was coming from was little comfort to Dominic. His flesh remained stubbornly resistant to reasoning.

Okay, so he'd always liked a sexual challenge in a woman, but this was ridiculous. This woman despised him. It was extremely perverse to desire someone who was making it blatantly obvious he would be the last man on earth she'd go to bed with.

'I repeat,' he stated forcibly. 'I only slept with Sarah the once. And I used protection. It was the last night of her employ as my secretary. Her boyfriend had just gone off with some other woman and Sarah was very upset.'

'So you *comforted* her,' Tina said, the most blistering sarcasm in her tone.

His eyes clashed with her coldly cynical gaze, and again, something happened within him. Something deep and dark and even more dangerous. For this time he could not even control his thoughts.

One day, madam, he vowed hotly, I'll make you look at me differently to that. One day you'll give me fire, not ice. *One* day!

The moment of mental madness was over as quickly as it had come. But it still rattled Dominic,

for it betrayed a lack of control previously unknown
to his character.

He really had to get a grip on this situation.

And his body.

Or was it his mind playing havoc with him?

No, no, not his mind. This woman.

'Something like that,' he grated out.

'Condoms have been known to fail, you know,' she
challenged tartly.

'Not the ones I buy.'

Her eyebrows lifted. Wickedly mocking, taunting
eyebrows. 'I know of no such infallible brand.'

Neither did Dominic. But he was not going to give
an inch where this woman was concerned.

'When and where can I take this test?' he asked,
determined to have done with this appalling scenario
as quickly as possible.

'I've rung the doctor,' his mother informed him.
'He said if you and Bonnie come in first thing on
Monday morning, he'll take the required blood tests
and have them sent off straight away. But, given it's
not an urgent criminal case, the results might take
anything up to a couple of weeks.'

'Surely they can do it quicker than that!'

'You can ask, I suppose. But I doubt it will make
any difference. Apparently there's a bit of a backlog,
due to increased demand for DNA tests, and they only
give priority to real emergencies. Police work and
such. Meanwhile, I've asked Tina and Bonnie to stay
here with us. She's been working and living in
Melbourne this past year and doesn't have anywhere
decent to stay in Sydney other than the little bedsit
Sarah was renting.'

'I don't think that's a very good idea, Mum,'

Dominic said firmly, gratified that he didn't sound as panic-stricken as he felt at this development.

'Why not?'

'For one thing, you'll grow attached to that baby in two weeks. How do you think you're going to feel when you find out she's not your granddaughter?'

She gave him a disturbingly smug look, as though she had some secret knowledge he wasn't privy to. 'I'll cope, *if* and when that happens. What other objections do you have?'

'I don't like to be pedantic, but you really know nothing about this woman, here, except what she's told you. For all you know, that baby in there could be anyone!'

Actually, this thought hadn't occurred to him before, but now that it had, he ran with it.

'And so could *she*!' he said, jabbing a finger towards the brunette. 'To invite a stranger into our home without checking her story with independent sources is not only naive, but downright stupid!'

CHAPTER FIVE

TINA'S eyes narrowed to dark slits at this last insult. Right, she thought savagely. This was war!

She'd put up with his looking at her as though he wanted to strangle her with his bare hands. She'd endured his huffing and puffing in pretend outrage. She'd even listened to his heated denials and unimaginative lies without actually laughing.

But this attack on *her* character and honesty was beyond the pale. First he'd called *Sarah* a liar, and now...now he was accusing *her* of the same. Worse! He was virtually calling her a shyster! She might have twisted the truth a little here today, but only because the truth was...well...complicated. Nothing changed the fact that this man *was* Bonnie's father. And now he was trying to worm his way out of accepting his responsibilities a second time!

'I had hoped to avoid bringing lawyers into this,' Tina flung at him in clipped tones, black eyes blazing. 'I'd hoped we could come to some amicable arrangement where Bonnie was concerned. But I see that was optimistic of me. I'm sorry, Mrs Hunter,' she said, turning to Bonnie's grandmother. 'I would have dearly liked to stay here with you. I can see you're not of your son's ilk. You're a good woman. But this is not going to work.'

'Oh, yes it will,' Mrs Hunter refuted strongly, and Tina blinked her astonishment. 'This is *my* house and I will have you here to stay if I want to. If you don't like it, Dominic, then you can be the one to go. Perhaps it's time you found a place of your own, anyway. The mortgages have long been paid off. And just think. If you lived on your own, you wouldn't have to worry about my matchmaking.'

Mortgages? Matchmaking?

Tina's eyebrows lifted. It seemed life in the Hunter household wasn't always smooth sailing.

'Fine,' the man himself snapped, and was actually whirling away when common sense returned to Tina. This was not what she wanted. Not at all!

'No, *wait*!' she said swiftly, and he stopped in mid-turn. 'Mrs Hunter, please,' she said pleadingly. 'I...I don't want to cause any trouble between you and your son.'

And she didn't. There was no advantage in it for her. Or for Bonnie. As much as she might like to tear strips off the man, it wasn't going to get her anywhere.

As for threatening to get a lawyer...she really didn't want to take that road, either. Court cases took time. And money.

Money she couldn't spare. Sarah's superannuation pay-out on her death had been a tidy little sum, but Tina had put that away in a special savings account for Bonnie's education. Her own savings were negligible. Acting wasn't the most steady or reliable of professions. Besides, she'd only been out of AIDA a year.

Common sense told Tina that conciliation was the way to go, not confrontation. She already had his mother on her side. Time to play a more clever and subtle hand.

It would almost kill her to back down, or make

compromising noises, but if Bonnie would eventually benefit, then she would do it.

Steeling herself, she harnessed her acting ability once more.

'Your son does have a point, Mrs Hunter,' Tina said with a convincing display of concession. 'I could be anyone. I do have my driver's licence and other ID with me, but I suppose that's not really enough. I dare say con-artists have such things all at the ready. Still, I can give you several phone numbers you can call to check out my identity. Friends. Employers. The legal aid lawyer who handled Sarah's will. I'm quite happy for you to have me checked out, Mr Hunter.'

She forced herself not to scowl at the man.

'As for Bonnie, I can certainly prove who *she* is. I brought her birth certificate with me. I also have the keys to Sarah's place, where there's a copy of her will and other personal papers which should help prove what I've told you and your mother today. I could get them and show them to you, if you like.'

He didn't exactly jump at her offer. In fact, he still looked decidedly reluctant. And remained grimly silent.

Tina sighed. So much for her humiliating herself. So much for compromise.

'Fair's fair, Dominic,' his mother intervened. 'Tina can't do much more than that, can she? Look, why don't you drive her over to Sarah's place tonight after dinner? That way you could start satisfying your doubts straight away and bring back anything Tina might need for herself and Bonnie at the same time.'

Tina saw the muscles along Dominic's strong jawline tighten appreciably. Clearly he didn't want to drive her anywhere. He didn't want to have anything to do with her.

Or with Bonnie.

Well, that was just too bad, she thought savagely.

Tina tried not to look as livid as she felt, but something must have shown in her face for his whole body seemed to stiffen, not just his jaw muscles.

It was probably her eyes. People often told her that her eyes gave her away every time. She'd tried to learn to control them, tried to make them project whatever emotion she wanted rather than what she was feeling at the time. An actress should be able to do that. But when she was this angry, when she disliked someone *this* much, she invariably failed.

'I'm not going to have any say in all this, am I?' the object of her intense dislike directed towards his mother, a black frustration in every word. 'Just don't blame me if things don't work out the way you hope they will.' He sucked in a deep breath which expanded his already large chest, then let it out slowly. 'I take it Joanna won't be coming for dinner tonight?'

'No,' his mother returned crisply. 'I postponed that till another night.'

'Well, thank heavens for small mercies,' he mocked. 'Who would have thought I'd be grateful to this fiasco for anything?'

Tina reacted poorly to the word 'fiasco'. But she bit her tongue. She had a feeling she was going to have to bite her tongue a lot around this man. He'd pressed the wrong buttons in her before she'd even met him. Dealing with him in the flesh stirred additional negative responses, not all of them strictly rational.

The truth was she'd never liked big men. Their size

sometimes unnerved her, making her feel small and defensive and vulnerable. Silly, really, when she was five foot nine inches tall and quite strong for her slender frame. But she'd often been grateful that most male actors were of the shorter, slighter variety.

Dominic Hunter was a big man. He looked extra big in this confined space, as opposed to his huge, airy office. Her gaze travelled up and down him as she assessed his actual height and weight. At least six foot four and a hundred kilos. Not fat, judging by his flat stomach, but with massive shoulders and long, strong arms. Large hands. Large fingers.

No doubt the rest of him was just as large.

Tina shuddered at the thought and he shot her a sharp glance. His hard blue eyes locked with hers, before dropping to her mouth, and then to her breasts.

Tina was flustered to find that her heart was racing madly.

Not that he was leering. He was simply subjecting her to the same cold appraisal she'd just given him. Tit for tat.

Immediately her chin shot up, her stomach clenching down hard in defiance of her unwanted and highly annoying inner turmoil. Be damned if she was going to start trembling in front of him like some nervous nelly!

But she was rattled all the same.

'I need to shower and change,' he said brusquely, and wrenched his gaze away from her breasts to land on his mother, who was watching her son with interest. 'Dinner still at the same time?' he rapped out.

'A little earlier, I think, since you're going out afterwards. June prepared everything this morning—thinking, of course, that I'd be having Joanna to dinner tonight. But Tina can eat Joanna's share. I just have to set the table and heat some things up. Say...seven-thirty?'

'Fine,' he muttered, and was gone, striding over to the stairs and swiftly disappearing from view. A door banged shut shortly afterwards and Tina let out a ragged sigh before she could think better of it.

Mrs Hunter reached over and patted her on the back of her hand. 'His bark's worse than his bite,' she said. 'Actually, I thought you handled the situation very well, standing up to him like that. Mentioning a lawyer was a very good idea. If there's one thing which will bring Dominic to heel it's the thought he might have to waste time fighting a paternity suit in court. He's a workaholic, you see, and workaholics never have time for anything else but work. It rather explains why he had an affair with your friend. The only woman he ever sees regularly is his secretary.'

'I don't think he's having an affair with his present secretary,' Tina said drily, and Mrs Hunter laughed.

'I'd have to agree with you there. I find it odd, though, that Dominic's so vehement in his denials over this affair. Why claim he only slept with Sarah the once if that wasn't so?'

Tina didn't like to call Dominic an out-and-out liar to his mother's face, but she had solid evidence he'd slept with Sarah more than once. 'Er...I'm not sure why he said that.'

'Could there have been another man?'

'Oh, no! Now that I *do* know. Sarah fell in love a lot, but only with one man at a time. She was in love with your son in late October, and even Dominic is admitting he slept with her towards the end of November. Believe me when I tell you there would have been no other man in the meantime. When Sarah loved, she loved exclusively and obsessively.'

'Fair enough. But why would Dominic say Sarah hadn't come to see him about the pregnancy if she had? My son is no saint, but he's usually honest.'

Clearly the woman couldn't embrace the fact her son could lie with the best of them.

'Um...I honestly can't say,' she murmured. 'Maybe he didn't want to look badly in your eyes. Look, I don't know what's going on in your son's mind, Mrs Hunter. But I know he's Bonnie's father and the DNA test will show that.'

'Oh, yes, I agree with you there. In fact, I have no doubts whatsoever!'

'You haven't?' Tina had begun to worry that Dominic's denials might have brought some doubt. She herself didn't have any, but she wasn't Dominic's mother.

'Heavens, no,' the woman said, smiling. 'Bonnie's the spitting image of Dominic when he was a baby. I noticed that straight away. Such a pretty child, he was. And a pretty lad too, till puberty turned him into the big lug he is today.'

Tina found it difficult to see any resemblance. She thought Bonnie looked like Sarah. Still, she hadn't known Dominic when he was a baby.

'Er...what do you think Dominic will do when the DNA test comes back and he can no longer deny he's the father?' Tina asked.

The woman sighed. 'I have to admit he won't be pleased. Hopefully, he'll come round.'

'I wonder if he will...'

Tina was gnawing at her bottom lip when she became aware of Mrs Hunter looking her over with an assessing gaze.

'Do you have a boyfriend, Tina?' she asked with seeming innocence, and Tina almost laughed. If Dominic Hunter's mother was thinking what Tina imagined she was thinking, then she'd better think again. Hell would freeze over before she fell for *that* man. Or any man, for that matter, she thought caustically.

Still, it was hardly the right moment to reveal what Sarah had always castigated her over: her inability to love or trust the opposite sex. Given both their backgrounds, Tina thought her negative attitude to the male species was justifiable. It amazed her that Sarah had always been so willing to be taken in by them.

Tina couldn't help being hard and cynical in her dealings with men, and sex. Not that she was a virgin. She'd slept with a couple of the species, though never for love. Simply to know how to act in sex scenes. She'd also wanted to see what all the hoo-ha was all about.

She still had no idea.

'No,' she denied. 'No boyfriend at the moment.'

The answer pleased Bonnie's grandmother.

'And is there any reason you *have* to return to Melbourne to live? You did say the part you were playing in that soap opera was over.'

'For the time being. But if the viewing public miss me, they might write me back in.'

'Can't you get an acting job here in Sydney?'

'Unfortunately there are more production companies in Melbourne.'

'Oh…'

'Please don't concern yourself, Mrs Hunter. Bonnie

is my number one priority at the moment, not my career. If you want me to stay in Sydney, I will.'

Actually, Tina was disillusioned with her choice of career at the moment. It wasn't bringing her the pleasure and satisfaction she'd once thought it would. She was more than happy to put acting aside for a while and look after Bonnie.

Mrs Hunter beamed, and Tina thought how lucky Bonnie was to have a grandmother like this.

'You know, you really must stop calling me Mrs Hunter. My name is Ida.'

'Ida,' Tina repeated, smiling.

'Wonderful. Now I suppose I'd better go get dinner ready before grumpy-bumps comes downstairs.'

Tina tried not to laugh, but 'grumpy-bumps' described Dominic Hunter to a T. Men like him didn't like women making waves in their lives. Clearly he was most put out by all this.

Tough, she thought.

'Can I be of any help?' she offered.

'Oh, no, dear, I'll be fine. Why don't you pop along to the powder room and freshen up for dinner?'

'Fine,' she said. 'I'll do just that.'

CHAPTER SIX

DOMINIC stepped under a deliberately cold shower, all the breath rushing from his lungs as the icy spray hit his seriously overheated flesh. Swearing, he gritted his teeth and stood there staunchly while the freezing water achieved what his will-power could not.

Finally, he turned the taps onto a warmer setting and reached for the shower gel, squirting several dollops into his hands, then lathering it all over his body, finding some satisfaction in having his hormones under control once again.

But for how long, with that female living under his roof?

Hell! He hadn't been the victim of such a wayward and unwanted burst of lust since he was fourteen!

Don't even *think* about her, he warned himself, when his flesh prickled once more.

But he *had* to think about her, *and* the situation.

Okay, so maybe it wasn't a scam, and maybe Tina wasn't a con-artist, but she was seriously deluded.

She had to be if she believed he was that baby's father.

Because it was impossible!

Well...not a hundred per cent impossible, he conceded reluctantly. Tina was right. Condoms had been known to fail. But the likelihood was extremely low. Besides, if Sarah had believed even for a moment he could be Bonnie's father, she *would* have come to see him.

But she hadn't!

No, Bonnie wasn't his child. Sarah had known that. Yet Tina believed he was.

Which meant Sarah had lied to her best friend.

Why did people lie? he speculated. Because of shame? To protect someone?

Perhaps the baby's father was a married man, someone who worked at Hunter & Associates...

Dominic frowned as he tipped his head back into the shower to let the soap wash free. He needed to find out the real father's identity—and quickly—before his own mother had time to get too attached to the child. And before he went stark raving mad!

My God, the thought of having that female under his roof for the next two weeks or more was too awful to contemplate. Those fantastic eyes of hers. That sulky, pouting mouth. Those small, high, firm breasts.

Dominic groaned. It seemed he only had to *think* about her now and he was in trouble. Reaching up, he snapped off the hot water tap and braced himself for more torture.

This time, the cold water didn't work nearly as quickly.

Twenty minutes later, dressed in too tight jeans and a navy golf shirt, a still agitated Dominic clomped downstairs. He hadn't bothered to shave, and a five o'clock shadow was beginning to sprout. His hair was still wet from his elongated shower and his tan loafers covered feet which looked like prunes, they'd been wet for so long.

At least dinner shouldn't be too bad, he conceded grudgingly as he strode along the hallway. He'd be sitting down, hidden from view. But he didn't fancy driving Tina anywhere afterwards. He didn't fancy being anywhere within touching distance of that woman!

He also didn't fancy having to keep defending himself to her when he was innocent. Damn it all, what had he done to deserve any of this? He'd been a good guy all his life, hadn't he? He'd been a good son. A good brother. A good friend. He didn't take drugs; didn't drink to excess; didn't cheat on his clients.

He worked hard and he gave money to charity.

Most important of all, he didn't indulge in heartless seductions and he *hadn't* impregnated any of his secretaries!

Hearing female voices coming from the kitchen on the right, Dominic turned left into the dining room, where he marched over to the sideboard and proceeded to pour himself a stiff shot of Scotch. There were times when only a drink would do!

'Don't drink that, Dominic.'

The glass froze just short of his mouth. He glared over at his mother as she walked in carrying a steaming soup tureen. 'Why?' he demanded to know.

'You have to drive after dinner, remember? And there's a bottle of your favourite red to have with the meal. You can't have both and be under the limit.'

'Then I'll only have one glass of wine,' he grated out, and took a deep swallow.

The alcohol hadn't had time to hit when Tina entered the room.

She'd put her hair up while he'd been upstairs, he noted. And glossed her mouth a tantalising pink. She looked as deliciously inviting to him as fairy-floss to a sugar-addicted child.

Her dark eyes glittered in his direction as she made her way to her seat at the table, their expression just short of scathing. Perversely, that seemed to be just what his body was waiting for.

Despairingly, Dominic jerked his eyes away from her and downed the rest of the whisky.

Tina watched him quaff back the drink as if he really needed it, but felt not the slightest twinge of sympathy for him. If ever there was a man who was acting guilty, it was Dominic Hunter.

His eyes were getting a hunted look to them, his body language betraying extreme annoyance which was way beyond the justified anger of the innocent. He was acting like some wild beast backed into a corner, practically quivering with the effort of controlling his frustration and suppressing his simmering fury.

Whenever he looked at her, Tina had the feeling he'd like nothing better than to grab hold of her and shake her till her teeth rattled. His appearance tonight didn't lessen his threatening air, either.

Out of his business suit he looked more like a construction foreman than ever. When he'd lifted that glass to his lips just now, his muscular bicep had bulged underneath the short sleeve. In fact, in that chest-hugging navy top and in those tight blue jeans, his whole body seemed to be bulging with menacing muscle.

The thought of being alone with him later was not a pleasant one.

Not that Tina seriously thought he would lay a finger on her. It was her own disquieting reaction to his macho size which was bothering her. Again.

Why couldn't he have been more like Sarah's usual boyfriends? came the irritable thought.

Perhaps because he *hadn't been* her boyfriend, shot back the highly disturbing answer.

Tina's eyes snapped up from the table to stare at Dominic as he settled himself opposite her. An unhappy frown creased her forehead as her mind grappled with this unexpected and unwanted thought.

What if he was telling the truth? What if he *had* only slept with Sarah the once? What if he *had* practised safe sex and Bonnie's father was really the mystery boyfriend Dominic claimed had dumped Sarah that week?

It was possible, Tina supposed. But, if so, then she was sitting at the wrong table, in the wrong home, with the wrong family.

No, I'm not, she refuted sternly in her mind, pushing away the split second of nausea. Sarah had told her personally that her boss, Dominic Hunter, was the man she was in love with, *and* sleeping with. There was also what Sarah had told her neighbour, as well as those cards from florists amongst Sarah's things, with all those intimate little messages, all signed 'D'. What were the odds on Sarah having two lovers working at Hunter & Associates with the initial D?

No, it had to be Dominic. Just because he wasn't Sarah's usual physical type that didn't let him off the hook. He was Bonnie's father all right.

Tina sighed her relief, dropped her eyes and started on with her soup.

Grumpy-bumps did the same, the meal progressing mostly in silence. Ida tried to make conversation, but Dominic refused to be drawn in. Tina didn't help much, she supposed, but, frankly, it was less stressful saying nothing and just eating.

Soup gave way to a veal dish done in a creamy sauce, followed by a thankfully fat-free fruit salad.

Tina had to watch what she ate. She was naturally slim, but television put ten pounds on you, and television was where the parts were at at the moment. She wasn't so foolish as to count her chickens before they hatched. As much as she might like to devote herself full-time to raising Bonnie, life just might not work out that way.

Tina was just finishing her fruit salad when a high-pitched cry infiltrated the dining room.

Tina immediately jumped up from the table. 'The baby!' she exclaimed, and dashed from the room.

Dominic rolled his eyes, which brought a sharp glance from his mother as she too rose from her seat.

'I'd get used to that sound, if I were you.'

'How many times do I have to tell you, Mum?' he said with a weary sigh. 'That baby is *not* mine.'

She laughed. She actually laughed. She was still laughing when she left the room.

Dominic shook his head after her. *Women,* he thought once again, with a wealth of frustration. They never gave up. There he'd been, actually worrying about his mother getting upset when she found out the baby *wasn't* her grandchild.

But she simply refused to be warned, refused to listen to reason—*and* her own son. She'd rather listen to the tissue of lies being fed to her by that perhaps well-meaning but seriously deluded creature.

The seriously deluded creature came back into the room, carrying a now silent pink bundle over her shoulder, patting what he supposed was the baby's back and making motherly noises.

'There, there, darling, yes, I know you're hungry and you're wet. I just need to...oh,' she cried on glancing around and seeing he was alone in the room. 'Where's Ida?'

'I have no idea,' he told her drily. 'I thought she'd gone to be with you and the baby.'

'I need to know where she put the disposable nappies she bought. Here! Why don't you hold your daughter while I go find her?'

Dominic's immediately horrified look brought an answering look of disgust. 'She won't bite, you know,' Tina snapped as she walked over and shoved the bundle into Dominic's startled arms. 'If she cries, just walk around the room and rock her backwards and forwards. She's a sucker for that.'

'But...but...'

But Tina was gone.

Dominic pressed his lips together and glared down at the baby lying in his stiffly outstretched arms. Two big blue eyes looked back up at him, two undeniably lovely and very engaging blue eyes. They showed no signs of any recent crying, which suggested a case of crocodile tears, undoubtedly the come-and-get-me-I'm-bored kind of crying.

'A little con-artist already, eh, kid?' he muttered. 'Just like your adopted mother. If she thinks this is going to work, then she can darned well think again!'

Startled by his deep male voice, that cute little baby face screwed up into a less cute expression and let rip.

Dominic's eyebrows hit the ceiling. How could so much noise come from such a sweet little bow-shaped mouth?

He was on his feet in a flash, pacing around the

room and rocking away like mad. He even resorted to some hopefully soothing small talk of his own.

'There, there, don't cry now. I didn't mean to make you cry. I'm not angry at you. It's this crazy situation I'm angry at. I guess you're not used to loud voices. Or men. I'll talk softly in future. I promise…'

All the pacing, rocking and promises didn't work. The cries got louder, if that were possible. Bunched little fists escaped the bunny rug she was wrapped in and starting flailing around like mad, hitting him once on the chin.

'I see you're not a natural-born father,' his mother said drily as she came in and took the baby from him. 'Let me show you.'

Lying the messy bundle down on the empty end of the dining table, she swiftly hooked those lethal weapons underneath the turned-in edges of the bunny rug, then wound the rug around very tight.

'Babies liked to be wrapped up tightly,' his mother lectured as she hoisted the papoose-like bundle up and over her shoulder. 'That way they feel safe and secure.'

All crying immediately ceased, two instantly dry blue eyes eyeing Dominic sanguinely from the safety of distance.

'See?' Ida said smugly.

'Yeah, I see,' came his dry reply. 'All females use tears to get what they want, right from the cradle. I'm going upstairs to make a phone call. Tell our guest to be ready to go in five minutes. I don't want to be all night doing this. It's already nine and I'm going out later.'

'Where to?'

He gave his mother a baleful look. 'Mum, I'm

thirty-three years old. I won't be grilled like some schoolboy. But, if you must know, I'm going to see my girlfriend.'

'Your *girlfriend*!'

'That's right.'

'But you've never mentioned having a girlfriend. At least…not lately.'

'I wonder why?' he said testily.

'I hate to think,' she retorted.

Dominic decided it was time to lay down the law. Unequivocally this time. He'd been a bit weak, letting his mother try to matchmake him with women like Joanna Parsons. He supposed he'd gone along with it in a fashion because he hadn't wanted to crush *all* her hopes at once. Mark decamping to a monastery had upset her a lot.

But enough was enough!

'Mum,' he stated firmly. 'You know my feelings about marriage and children. They're not for me. Look, I know you think I'm going to change my mind about that one day, but I won't. I know you think I'm going to fall in love one day, but I won't.'

'Does this girlfriend of yours know that?' she asked archly.

'She certainly does.'

'Strange girlfriend.'

'Shani understands me. We have an…arrangement.'

'Meaning you just use each other for sex.'

Dominic winced. 'I wouldn't put it quite that crudely.'

'Then how would you put it?'

'We're…lovers.'

'No, you're not. Love has nothing whatsoever to do with what you do with each other.'

His mother's scorn stung. Dominic also resented being made to feel ashamed of what was really a very practical and sensible relationship. He wasn't hurting anyone, least of all Shani.

'That's a very old-fashioned viewpoint,' he snapped, and swung round to leave the room, only to find Tina standing in the doorway, a bottle in one hand and a nappy in the other.

How much had she overheard? he wondered.

If the shock in her eyes was any judge, then everything about his relationship with Shani.

'If you'll excuse me,' he ground out as he approached the doorway.

She stepped aside with a speed and a flash of panic in her eyes which was downright insulting. What did she think? That physical contact with him would contaminate her?

Dominic almost laughed. She'd have a right to be scared if she knew what he'd been thinking and feeling about her all through dinner.

Fortunately, those feelings seemed to have taken a temporary back seat. Perhaps because he'd decided to take positive action to rid himself of them, once and for all!

He strode on down the hallway, then mounted the stairs two at a time.

Five minutes later he walked more sedately back downstairs, his equilibrium restored, his temper well under control. Shani would be waiting for him, regardless of when he arrived.

Sensible, sexy Shani.

If only there were more women like her!

CHAPTER SEVEN

TINA sat stiffly and silently in the passenger seat of Dominic Hunter's plush and new-smelling car, trying desperately to ignore the undermining and somewhat confusing feelings flooding through her.

She'd known it would not be a pleasant experience being alone with this man in the confines of a car.

But it wasn't his broad shoulders bothering her at that moment. It was something which had happened when she'd overheard his tiff with Ida in the dining room.

As she'd listened to Dominic Hunter admitting to a strictly sexual relationship with some secret girl-friend, she'd experienced the strangest reaction.

Not contempt, as one might have imagined.

But a weird kind of excitement.

Excitement, for pity's sake!

Tina had been so shocked that she'd stood rooted to the spot, her mouth half open, her heart racing with a dark rush of adrenaline. Her mind had instantly flooded with the most appalling erotic pictures, involving not him and this Shani woman, but herself!

When he'd started striding towards where she was standing in the doorway, she hadn't been able to get out of his way quickly enough.

Fifteen minutes later, she was still in shock, even more so because those disturbing feelings hadn't abated. If anything, they'd grown worse. She was pricklingly aware of her own body as she sat in the car so close to him. And awesomely aware of his!

Tina could not understand what was happening to her. She didn't like big men, for starters. And she didn't like sex at all!

'Tell me about your friendship with Sarah,' he said abruptly into the tortured silence.

'Why?' she burst out, angry with him for doing this to her. 'What's the point?'

'No point,' he grumped. 'Just something to talk about. It'll take us at least half an hour to get over the bridge and out to Sarah's place. You did say Lewisham, didn't you?'

'Yes,' she muttered.

Lewisham was an inner western suburb which straddled the railway line and was full of old blocks of flats, plus old houses cut up into small apartments and bedsits. Sarah had rented one of the latter. It was cramped, but clean, and possibly all she'd been able to afford on her single mother's allowance.

'Well?' he prompted impatiently.

Tina shrugged. Why not tell him? He would have to know in the end. Sarah was the mother of his child, after all. And it was better than sitting there thinking thoughts she'd much rather not think.

So she told him. And she didn't bother to water anything down. She told him the whole unvarnished, unsavoury truth.

It was blessedly distracting, watching his initial shock to her sordid tale, then trying to guess his thoughts and reactions.

There was no doubting he could hold a superb poker face when he wanted to. She had no idea what he was really thinking.

To give him credit, he didn't pass any superficial judgements, or express any false sympathies. When she'd finished the first part of her story, his questions weren't cruel, just inquisitive.

'So when the terrace house burnt down that night, killing both your mothers and several...er...guests, where were you and Sarah?'

'Out.'

'*Out?* In the middle of the night up at the Cross?'

Tina shrugged. 'Better than staying at home. A ship was in port and our mums had brought home quite a party. They'd all had a lot to drink, and when that happened I knew to keep Sarah out of harm's way. Even at nine, Sarah was attracting male attention.'

'Good God. At *nine*?'

He fell silent, as though having difficulty absorbing such an unimaginable lifestyle. Tina had no such difficulty. She'd lived it. And she'd lived the difficult years after their mothers had died, when she'd still had to protect Sarah from the opposite sex.

It had been hard when Sarah herself had been such a willing victim, right from her early teenage years. As much as she regretted it now, Tina understood why she'd walked out of Sarah's life. She simply hadn't been able to stand by and watch Sarah being used any more. She'd had enough!

'So where did you and Sarah go after the fire?' came the next question.

'We became wards of the state.'

'What about your grandparents?'

'Never knew them. After our mothers died, the welfare people must have searched. Maybe they found them, but obviously, at the time, they didn't want anything to do with the offspring of their black sheep daughters. You see, both our birth certificates said 'fathers unknown'. By the time *we* were old enough to search, Sarah's grandparents were dead and she had no aunts and uncles. I discovered a grandfather and three uncles living in England. I wrote several times. One of my uncles eventually wrote back to tell me that my letters had upset my grandfather very much, that my mother had been a bad seed, who'd brought the family nothing but shame and misery, and they would appreciate it if I didn't write or contact them ever again.'

'That must have been tough.'

'Life isn't meant to be easy, I'm told,' she said caustically, happy to be back to her old, cynical, hard-hearted self.

Thinking about her past was always a sobering experience. It didn't leave much room for any other feelings besides bitterness. How she could have even momentarily succumbed to such a crazy thing as sexual desire for the man sitting next to her was beyond her! She knew better than anyone what men were like, especially where sex was concerned.

'Anyway, back to Sarah and me,' she went on, quite coldly. 'Neither of us could be legally adopted because there were no parents to sign the papers. We were both fostered out once, but that didn't work too well. The darling man of the house couldn't keep his hands off Sarah. I complained to the authorities and, after another equally disastrous placement, they just kept us in a home they had for wards of the state. We went to the local school during the day, but neither of us excelled. Not that we were dumb, but Sarah was too busy chatting up the boys and I was off in a world of my own. As soon as we were fifteen, we left school and got jobs serving in shops. Sarah did a secretarial course at night, and worked her way up to better and better positions, while I did any old job and furthered my education. We flatted together till last year, when I went to Melbourne to find work.'

No way was she going to tell him about their argument and estrangement.

'What kind of work?'

'Didn't your mother tell you?'

'Tell me what?'

'I'm an aspiring actor.'

'No, she didn't tell me. So are you a good actor?'

'I graduated from AIDA.'

'Mmm. I hear that's a very difficult course to get in to.'

'It is. I auditioned every year for three years before I won a place.'

'Driving ambition or just plain stubborn?'

'I would have once said driving ambition. Now I lean towards just plain stubborn.'

'I can believe that,' he said drily. 'And did you find yourself a good acting job in Melbourne?'

'That depends on how you look at it. I got regular work on a soap playing a *femme fatale* who unfortunately was written out at the end of the season. Some people look down on doing soaps, but they're a good showcase if you have talent. And it's something to put in my rather thin resumé.'

'So what's going to happen to your acting career now you have Bonnie to look after?'

'It'll just have to take a back seat for a while.'

'How old are you, by the way?'

'Twenty-six. Why?'

'What's your money situation like?' he asked, ignoring her 'why'.

'Is this just curiosity or are you planning on making a charitable donation?' she flung at him caustically.

'Stop being stroppy and just answer the question.'

Stroppy, was she? She hadn't *begun* to be stroppy! 'My financial status is my own private and personal business. You don't honestly think I'd give such information to a man I might have to sue, do you?'

'Meaning you're not exactly flush, otherwise you'd throw it in my face.'

'Meaning you and I are enemies, Mr Hunter. I won't be supplying you with any knowledge which might give you an advantage over me. Sarah was the sweetest, softest person in the entire world and she's entrusted me with her daughter. Believe me when I tell you I aim to do anything and everything in my power to force you to accept her as such, and to provide for her, for *life*, in the manner she deserves.'

'So money's the bottom line, is that it?'

'God, but I pity you. *Love's* the bottom line, you fool. I love Bonnie, but I'm not her blood. You and your mother are. Ida can give Bonnie the kind of love I can't give her, and which a child always craves. Believe me, I know. I don't delude myself *you'll* ever give your daughter love. From what I've heard and seen of you, you're impervious to the emotion. But money can provide a child with the illusion of love. And who knows? In time, you might grow to care for Bonnie. If she's anything like her mother in nature— and I suspect she is—it will be hard not to.'

'Don't you think this lecture would be best left till the DNA test comes back?'

'You wanted me to talk about Sarah,' she retorted.

'I can't talk about Sarah without bringing up Bonnie. Not to mention Bonnie's defunct father!'

'Since you feel so strongly—and so angrily—about my supposed part in all this, why didn't you come and see me sooner? When Sarah told you that I denied being Bonnie's father and gave her money for an abortion, why didn't you come flying into my office like an avenging angel back then? The woman who barged into my life today would not have shrunk from such an action. Why wait till now?'

Tina hadn't been anticipating this question and it flustered her for a moment. 'Well, I...I...I was in Melbourne, remember?'

'Surely you came back to see Sarah when Bonnie was born?'

Tina coloured guiltily as she felt him staring at her. 'Actually, no...I...I didn't,' she confessed, a lump forming in her throat.

There was a short, sharp silence.

'Are you going to tell me why?' he asked, sounding puzzled and almost angry. 'Or are you going to leave me to think you're the strangest kind of best friend God ever put breath into?'

'I...we...we'd argued,' Tina choked out, and looked away from him and out through the passenger window. They were approaching the Harbour Bridge at the time, but Tina saw nothing of the spectacular view. She was busy battling for control.

'What about?' he demanded to know.

She could not speak. She just shook her head at him as tears flooded her eyes.

He sighed. 'There are tissues in the glove-box.'

She'd just retrieved a handful when her long-held

grief and guilt broke free and she burst into deep, gut-wrenching sobs.

Dominic was grateful he was driving across the bridge at the time. For he could not stop, or pull over to the side. Thank the Lord he could not do anything really stupid like take her into his arms.

He did have to eventually slow down for the toll gates. But his stop was only minimal. Even so, the man collecting the money glowered at him as if he was some heartless bastard for making his woman cry like that.

The sound of her weeping moved him more than he liked, as had her story of her wretched upbringing. It explained a lot about her, and her determination to give Sarah's child the best. It also sparked a weird guilt in him which he couldn't fathom, or reason with. Perhaps it came with her accusation that he was incapable of loving or caring for a person.

Finally her sobs quietened, and she straightened in the seat, the no doubt sodden tissues still clenched tightly in her lap.

'Better now?' he asked gently.

She nodded.

'Would you like to talk about it? Your argument with Sarah?'

'Not really,' she said tautly.

'Fair enough. I presume you were still in Melbourne when she was killed?'

Again, she nodded, her hands twisting in her lap.

'You hadn't made up after your argument?' he probed.

She looked pained at this question. 'I...I tried to call her several times. But she'd left her job and moved out of our old flat. Her name wasn't in the directory. She didn't have a phone, you see. I knew she knew where *I* was, so I thought...I thought she didn't want to have anything further to do with me...'

'Did you think she'd had an abortion?'

Her eyes flashed round, still luminous from her tears, but filled with outrage. 'Sarah would *never* have had an abortion!'

'Fair enough. Don't overreact, now. I'm just trying to figure this out. I thought you might have argued over her not having an abortion. I mean...I would imagine a girl of your unhappy background might not agree with bringing an unwanted child into the world.'

'Then it just shows you know nothing whatsoever about girls like me. Or girls at all, for that matter. If you must know, we argued about *you*!'

'*Me?*' He could not have been more shocked.

'That's right. Look, you have to understand Sarah's life-long behaviour with men to know why I reacted as badly as I did. She was forever falling in love, often with men she worked with, and never with men who loved her back. I'd grown so tired of picking up the pieces after her latest affair had blown up in her face. I was also sick and tired of her having to change jobs because she'd become involved yet again in some sordid affair with a married man.'

'She had affairs with married men?'

'Sometimes. Look, she wasn't a slut or anything like that. She just couldn't resist being loved. If a man told her he loved her then she simply could not resist him. It wasn't sex she wanted, but love. When she went to work for Hunter & Associates she promised me it would be different. But I soon began to see the signs that she was in love again. The hours she took getting ready for work. The new clothes. The sexy perfume. So I tackled her on who the new man was. Initially she denied being involved with anyone at work, but I knew she was. I wouldn't let it drop. When she finally confessed to me she was in love with you, her new boss, I just saw red.'

'Sarah was in love with me?' Dominic repeated, stunned.

'Please don't pretend you didn't know that,' came her scathing remark.

'But I didn't! I swear to you.'

'Maybe she hid the depth of her feelings from you because she knew the sort of man you were,' she suggested scornfully. 'Who knows now? Anyway, I tore strips off her, called her a fool and, yes, I called her a slut. All the usual insults between friends. She defended her love for you with such passion, said it was deeper than anything she'd ever felt before. She even called *me* the fool because I didn't know what love was.'

Tina's sigh sounded so sad, and full of regret. 'Things were said that shouldn't have been said, I guess. I was already packed to go to Melbourne for a while. Sarah told me to get out and that she didn't want to see or hear from me ever again.'

'I see,' Dominic murmured, while his mind raced, this more in-depth perspective on Sarah disturbing his till now confident stance over his being Bonnie's father.

That night he'd slept with her...had she lied about the mystery boyfriend? Had she contrived a situation where he'd feel sorry for her and take her into his arms? Had she skilfully engineered a seduction scene, undermining his will-power with wine before going in for the kill with the oldest trick in the book? Tears!

If she had, then for what purpose?

There really was only one possible answer.

To entrap him with a pregnancy...

His mind searched that night for exactly what had happened, but in all honesty he was a bit fuzzy about the details. It was so long ago, and he'd had quite a bit to drink that night.

Still, he was absolutely sure they'd used protection both times.

Both times?

His stomach crunched down hard at this sudden added memory. Sarah had snuggled up to him during the night and aroused him again with a very seductive and experienced hand. It had been *she* who'd put the condom on him that second time, now that he came to think of it. Had she done something to it? Had she hoped in her one-sided and silly love that she might conceive and that he would subsequently marry her?

From what Tina had told him, the girl had been a hopeless romantic, a needy, neglected soul who'd craved affection and sought it in all the wrong places.

She certainly didn't find it in *you*, then, came the brutal and uncomfortable thought.

The next morning, he'd made it quite clear that the night before had been a mistake and a oncer. He'd taken her distressed silence for embarrassment and agreement, whereas maybe it had been the futility of her feelings sinking in. Maybe, when she'd found out she was pregnant, she'd been loath to come to him and admit her trickery.

Which brought him right back to one of Tina's original accusations: that Sarah had come to him with news of her pregnancy and that he'd denied paternity and given her money for a termination.

Some more pennies dropped, and he shot Tina a bewildered look. 'You didn't even know she was pregnant, did you?'

'No,' she muttered.

Dominic's temper shot up. 'In that case, how could she have told you she'd come to me after she found out about the baby? Hell on earth, you lied about that, didn't you?'

He watched her shoulders straighten, her eyes once again hard and cold. 'Only in so many words. The fact still remains she did just that. She told her new neighbour all about it, and that woman related the whole sorry episode to me only yesterday. She said Sarah cried and cried for days afterwards.'

Dominic could not believe what he was hearing. 'You condemned me on second-hand hearsay?'

She flashed him a look of utter scorn. 'No. I have *other* damning evidence against you.'

'What other evidence?'

'Never you mind.'

'But I *do* mind,' he bit out. 'I mind very much indeed.'

'And I mind your letting Sarah down,' she lashed out. 'Whether you loved her or not, you could at least have supported her, both emotionally and financially. It breaks my heart to think of her having that baby all alone, and her dying all alone.'

'What breaks your heart, madam,' he countered savagely, 'is that *you* let her down. You weren't there when she needed you. You called her a silly slut and left her to fend for herself when you knew she wasn't nearly as strong as you were.'

Her face went dead white in the dim light of the car, and Dominic wished with all his heart that he could take the nasty words back again.

'Don't you dare cry again!' he ground out when her chin started quivering. They were far too close to the address she'd given him. Far too close to his stopping the car and having no excuse not to extend her some physical sympathy.

Immediately her chin stopped trembling, and she blazed black fury at him.

Hell, but she was something to behold when she was in a rage. Her face flushed. Her eyes flashed. And those lovely full lips of hers alternately pressed and pouted.

'I'll never cry in front of you again, you unconscionable bastard!' she pronounced.

Thank heaven for more small mercies, he thought ruefully as he turned off Parramatta Road and headed for the bridge which crossed the railway line and led to their destination.

CHAPTER EIGHT

THE house looked just as shabby at night as it did in daylight, Tina thought as she led Dominic down the side path to the door which led into Sarah's bedsit. Tina still cringed at the sight of it.

It had probably been a grand old residence once, many years before someone had bought it and divided it into several flats and bedsits. Time and neglect now saw the roof and guttering badly in need of repair. The paint was peeling from the old wooden window-frames. Some of panes were cracked. The garden was overgrown; the paths were full of weeds.

Tina unlocked the door and snapped on the light, once again feeling overwhelmed with sadness at Sarah being forced to live in a place like this with her baby. Maybe it would do Dominic Hunter good to see what the mother of his child had been reduced to.

He didn't say a word as he glanced around the wretched room which had been Sarah and Bonnie's home. Tina glanced around again as well, looking past the surface cleaniless to the harsh reality beyond.

The paint on the wall was cracked and peeling. The rug on the floor was threadbare. A cheap plastic light fitting covered the bare bulb in the ceiling. All the furniture was shabby and second-hand, except for the quilt on the bed and the things Sarah had bought for the baby. Now *they* were all brand, spanking new, and quite expensive.

How like Sarah, Tina had thought when she'd first

walked in here just over a week ago. Only the best for her baby.

At the time, she'd wondered how Sarah had afforded to buy the imported cradle and pram and Bouncinette, not to mention the expensive baby outfits. Sarah had never been one to save. She'd spent everything she'd earned every week on her appearance, spending a fortune on clothes and accessories, not to mention make-up and visits to the hairdresser.

Tina had discovered the answer to that particular riddle when she'd looked in the battered wardrobe and discovered all Sarah's own lovely clothes had gone, replaced by a few cheap outfits. The dressing table drawers had revealed a similar dearth of personal possessions. All her jewellery had gone, along with her collection of leather handbags and designer scarves.

The dressing table top was bare of any feminine frippery, only one small photo of Sarah and Bonnie propped against the mirror.

The old lady in the adjoining bedsit—the one who'd supplied the information about Sarah's disastrous visit to Dominic—had confirmed that Sarah had sold everything she could to outfit her precious baby girl. It seemed Sarah had known the sex of the baby from the time of her ultrasound at four months, a couple of months after she'd come here to live. Apparently she'd left Hunter & Associates early in her pregnancy because she'd been too sick to work.

This last piece of information had upset Tina as well. If only she'd known, she'd have been on the first plane back to Sydney.

'You've been staying here?' Dominic asked at last, his expression almost disbelieving.

'Yes,' she replied defensively. Where else? 'They're my two suitcases against the wall.' Still with her things in them. She hadn't wanted to unpack. She hadn't planned on staying too long.

'Then don't go trying to bluff me about having money,' he snapped. 'Come on, collect what you need so we can get the hell out of here. I've seen some depressing places in my life but this wins hands down. Believe me when I tell you if Sarah *had* come to me and told me she was pregnant, she and her baby wouldn't have had to live like this!'

Tina stared at him as the most bewildering confusion claimed her. For he sounded so sincere. And genuinely upset.

'She really didn't come to see you?' she found herself asking.

'No,' he said, and looked her straight in the eye without wavering. 'The morning after she stopped working for me was the last time I saw Sarah. I never even ran into her in the lift after that. To be brutally honest, I didn't even realise she'd left the company.'

'But *why* would she say she'd been to see you if she hadn't?'

'I have no idea. Who was it who told you that?'

'The old lady who lives in the next bedsit.'

'What's her name?'

'What? Oh…er…Betty. I don't know her second name.'

'I see. Well, maybe Sarah told her she was coming to see me, but then changed her mind. Maybe when this Betty asked her what happened, she made up a little white lie out of embarrassment. I don't think we'll ever know what really happened, or what was going through her mind at the time.'

'I guess not,' Tina said wearily, and sat down on the edge of the bed. The mattress sagged, as did her shoulders. 'What does it matter now, anyway?'

'It matters to me when people call me a liar,' Dominic ground out. 'I'm no saint, Tina, but I'm not an unconscionable bastard, either.'

She winced at her words, well aware the insult had been flung more out of shame than genuine belief in his total wickedness. It was *she* who'd felt wicked at the time. Wicked and way, way out of control.

She glanced up at him, and tried to be fair.

Because let's face it, Tina, her conscience demanded, you haven't been fair to him all day. Before you even met the man you were right and ready to accuse. And not to listen. You played the avenging angel role to a T, and gave Sarah saintly qualities which she didn't have.

The truth was Sarah had used to lie quite a bit, whenever she'd thought the truth might get her into trouble, or into an argument. Sarah had hated to confront, or be confronted. She'd always taken the line of least resistance.

'I...I'm sorry I said that,' she muttered.

'And I'm sorry I said you let Sarah down,' he returned, more gently than she deserved. 'From what I've seen, she couldn't have asked for a better friend. Or a better mother for her baby.'

'Oh,' Tina choked out, her chin wobbling while tears filled her eyes.

'You vowed you'd never cry in front of me again!' he warned sharply.

'I...I can't help it,' she sobbed, her hands flying up to cover her face as the tears spilled over.

*   *   *

Dominic stared at her in horror.

Why me? he agonised.

He grimaced at the sight of her shaking shoulders, then groaned at the sounds of her heartfelt sobs, torn by his natural male urge to offer comfort to a weeping woman, yet worried sick over what might overtake him once he touched her.

Look what had happened the last time he'd gathered a crying female in his arms! And Sarah hadn't even been his type!

Tina, however, was very definitely his type.

And *how*!

He was standing there at a safe distance when the thought occurred to him that he was worrying for nothing, because *he* wasn't *Tina's* type!

There really was little danger of anything untoward happening when the woman in your arms couldn't stand a bar of you.

That apology of hers just now had been nothing but a grudging concession. She still believed he was a liar and a heartless seducer.

Reassured, Dominic walked over and sat down on the narrow bed beside her, sending the ancient mattress into a dangerous dip which instantly propelled Tina hard against his side.

'Oh!' she gasped, her hands flying away from her face in panic.

'It's all right,' he said gruffly, and curved an arm around her shoulders.

But it wasn't all right. Everything was all wrong.

The way she was looking at him for starters, her eyes wide and lustrous. The way her face remained upturned, with her lips invitingly parted. The way her hands fluttered against his chest then remained there, faintly trembling.

Dominic gave her a chance. He really did. She could have wrenched away from him, could have stopped him at any point during the time it took for his free hand to lift and capture that quivering chin with his fingers.

But she didn't struggle, or stop him. She just stared up into his eyes, her lips gasping even further apart when his mouth began to descend.

Tina knew he was going to kiss her. She *knew*, but she did nothing, said nothing.

She let his lips cover hers without protest. Let his tongue slide deep into her mouth. Let his hand slide down her neck and over one of her treacherously throbbing breasts.

This is madness, was her last coherent thought, before a wild explosion of desire blew her brain apart, skittering all common sense and evoking in its place the most urgent need. Her arms slid up around his neck and she was pulling him down, down onto the bed with her.

Dominic had little time to feel shock at her wild response. If his mind momentarily questioned her unexpected passion, his body didn't. His own arousal soared, tipping him over that edge on which he'd balanced precariously all evening.

Tina moaned when he stopped kissing her to lift her up onto the pillow. She moaned again when he pushed her legs apart and fell upon her once more, his mouth crashing back down on hers, his hard, heavy body pressing her deep into the mattress.

She felt as if she was drowning, with no air for her lungs. Her head was spinning wildly. But she didn't care. What a delicious death, she thought, and wrapped her arms even tighter around his neck.

He twisted slightly to one side, but this time he didn't stop the kissing. She felt his hand on her body, as hot and hungry as his mouth as it stroked roughly down her chest before scooping up underneath her top to where her braless breasts were waiting for him, aching and tense. Everything inside her contracted when his hands grazed over her exquisitely erect nipples, a moan of raw pleasure echoing deep in her throat.

Men had touched her breasts before, but never like this, never with such a wild, uncontrollable ardour. There was no finesse in his questing fingers, just naked animal passion as he squeezed the sensitive peaks over and over and left them aching for more.

When his mouth wrenched away and his hand slid down from her breasts, she cried out with dismay. No, don't stop, don't stop, came the almost despairing but silent plea.

But he wasn't stopping.

She watched, eyes wide and lungs heaving, as he pushed up her top and slid down to put his mouth where his hands had been.

His tongue and teeth were as merciless as his fingers, laving and nipping at her nipples till they felt like pokers hot from a fire. She couldn't get enough, arching her back and pressing them up into his face for more. She even liked it when he rubbed his stubbly chin over their burning peaks, gasping as spears of the most delicious sensation darted all through her body.

Her eyes squeezed shut, perhaps in denial of the dizzying pleasure of it all. But Tina found no safe haven in the darkness. If anything, being unable to see what he was doing enhanced the experience, sharpening her awareness of her body and its responses. Her breasts had never felt so swollen, or so exquisitely sensitive. Her body had never felt so restless, so craving.

His abrupt abandonment of her needy, greedy flesh sent her eyes flying open.

He was kneeling back on his haunches between her outstretched legs, his dark head bent over, his hands reaching for the button at her waistband. Somewhat dazedly, she stared down at the sight she made lying there, semi-naked, her top bunched up around her neck, her breasts bare, her nipples still wet and tingling.

Dominic started peeling the tight stretch pants down from her hips, taking her G-string with them, bending to kiss her quivering stomach as he did so.

Groaning, she twisted her head to one side, and might have closed her eyes again, ready to wallow in whatever he did to her, when her dilated gaze encountered the small photograph of Sarah and Bonnie on the dressing table.

The erotic haze which had been enslaving Tina so totally immediately lifted. If someone had thrown a bucket of iced water on her, the effect could not have been more dramatic.

Instant coldness where a moment before there had been the most blistering heat. A crippling dismay in place of that incredible desire.

'Oh, God...*no*!' she cried out, and sat bolt-upright, pushing him back off the bed with an adrenaline-induced burst of strength. He staggered to his feet, then just stood there, staring at her while she frantically pulled down her top, then started yanking up the tight white pants. It was difficult, but she managed. Finally, she swung her feet over the side of the bed and might have bolted for the door, but she started shaking. So she just sat there, hugging herself as great tremors raced all through her.

When Dominic went to sit down beside her, she froze him with her eyes.

'Don't you d...dare come near me,' she warned, her teeth still chattering. 'Or t...t...touch me ever again.'

'Tina, for pity's sake! Be fair. You wanted me to. You know you did.'

She shook her head violently. 'No, I d...d...didn't. I didn't *want* you to. You're the last man on earth I'd want making love to me. I hate and d...despise you.'

'But why? I thought you believed me about Sarah now.'

Tina gritted her teeth, using every ounce of will she possessed to stop shaking and face this man. 'You still used and abused her,' she bit out. 'You didn't love her but you made love to her anyway. Then, when she stopped working for you, you just moved on to that...that Shani person. I wonder if *she* knows the sort of man she's tangled up with. A cold-blooded sex machine, that's what you are. Oh, you know the right moves all right. And you certainly know when to strike: when a girl is at her lowest emotionally, tired and vulnerable and sick at heart. That's when you move in for the kill, isn't it? You...you...callous, unfeeling pig!'

Her tirade over, Tina buried her face in her hands and dissolved into distressed tears.

Dominic had never felt worse in his whole life.

Physically and emotionally.

The fiercest frustration raged, along with remorse and guilt and, yes, confusion.

In one way he was glad she'd stopped him. Because he would not have been able to stop himself. He would have continued on. Without any thought of the consequences. Without a condom.

Such a reality was as alien to him as it was bewildering. What was it about this woman which made him lose all control and common sense? Was it just a matter of a unique chemistry, or could something else be at work here, that age-old emotional trap which made fools of men and which Dominic had sworn never to fall victim to?

He shook his head in denial of this last possibility. Surely falling in love took longer than this!

Still, as he stared at the wretched figure hunched on the bed a huge wave of tenderness flooded through him. He just had to go to her. Had to make things right. Had to.

He knelt down at her knees and took her hands in his, holding them tight even while she tried to wrench them away.

'No, you must listen to me,' he said firmly. 'You've had your say. Now let me have mine.'

She glared at him with daggers in her tear-filled eyes.

'I didn't mean for that to happen. I didn't really

want it, either, or plan it. But the truth is I've been attracted to you since I first set eyes on you in my office.

'Yes, it's true,' he insisted when he saw the disbelief in her eyes. 'I couldn't get you out of my mind. I've always been attracted to slender, dark-eyed brunettes. Then, when I came home and found you there, my brain and body started a war which has been going on ever since. I was as angry with you as you were with me. Because I *hadn't* done what you accused me of. But at the same time I kept wanting to pull you in my arms and make mad, passionate love to you. To be brutally honest, I had an erection all through dinner.'

Her dark eyes rounded and her lips fell tantalisingly apart. It took all of his will-power not to close the relatively short distance between their mouths once more.

He suspected he could seduce her even now, if he were ruthless enough. But Dominic didn't want that. He wanted more from this woman than just her body. He wanted her respect as well.

And she didn't respect him at the moment. Not one iota.

'I think you're attracted to me too,' he added, and waited for her to deny it.

She didn't, and his heart began to beat faster, his mind already racing to the time when he would have her again under him on a bed. He would not let her stop him the next time. He would use every erotic skill he'd ever learned to keep her there till they were both satisfied. Not once, but over and over!

It's just lust, he realised abruptly with a great whoosh of relief. Hell, for a moment there...

'There's nothing wrong with us being friends, is there?' he suggested reasonably. 'If it turns out I'm Bonnie's father, then surely it would be best all round if we got on well.'

'You're…you're admitting you could be Bonnie's father?'

'It's possible, I suppose,' he said, though privately Dominic brushed aside this slim possibility as not worth worrying about, certainly not till the test results came back. He saw little point in facing a problem till it really existed. Still, if admitting he might be Bonnie's father would get him into Tina's good books…

'What about the mystery boyfriend?' she said, wariness in her voice. 'Or are you admitting he doesn't exist?'

'He exists all right. I intend to find him myself.'

'Best look in the mirror, then.' She extricated her hands from his and gave him a cold look. 'As for our being…*friends*,' she scoffed. 'I can't see that happening. Now that I know what I'm dealing with I'll be on guard, believe me.'

Dominic stood up and did his best to keep reasonably calm in the face of her ongoing scorn. It was one step forward and three steps backwards with this woman. 'What do you mean…what you're dealing with?'

'You know exactly what I mean,' she snapped. 'You're a predator, Dominic. A taker. You think you can have any woman you want. I'm sure there are countless scores on your gun. But don't mark a notch for me, because I'm not like Sarah or Shani or any of the other poor creatures you've used and discarded. I might have seemed like one tonight, but everyone's entitled to one error in judgement. I underestimated you, and I overestimated myself. I didn't realise I could be got at that way. Now I know differently.'

'I don't believe this!' He spun away and began to pace agitatedly around the room. She was doing it to him again, making him feel a heel when he'd bent over backwards to be reasonable. Hell, anyone would think that wanting to make love with a woman was a capital offence!

Her glance was scathing as she stood up. 'I'm sure after you've visited your Shani later tonight you'll feel much better. After all, one slender, dark-eyed brunette is pretty much like another to a man like you!'

Her sarcasm stung him to the quick, bringing an angry flush to his face. 'I'll have you know that Shani is a very intelligent woman, with a mind of her own. I do not use her, any more than she uses me.'

'How nice. Then you're well suited, aren't you?'

'Too right.'

'Then leave me alone in future.'

'Don't worry. I will!'

CHAPTER NINE

IT WAS just on eleven when Shani let a still fuming
Dominic into her apartment. Normally Dominic
wouldn't have got past the small foyer before the sex
started. This time he stalked past Shani and went
straight for the cabinet in the living room where she
kept her hard liquor and clean glasses.

'Bad day, darling?' she drawled as he slopped
some Scotch into a glass.

He grunted, then quaffed back the lot.

She came up behind him and slid her hands over
his already tense shoulders in a seductive fashion. His
fingers stiffened around the glass as her hands slid
down his arms then snaked around his waist before
travelling lower.

'Mmm,' she said with salacious pleasure.

Confusion crashed through him as his conscience
screamed at him not to do this. This is all wrong! It's
Tina you're wanting. Not Shani.

But Tina despises you, the devil tempted. You'll
never have her in your bed. Never! You can't walk
around like this for ever. You'll go insane. And it's
not as though Shani minds.

With a tortured groan he whirled, scooped her up
into his arms and carried her into the bedroom. Five
minutes later, a stunned Shani was pulling the sheet
up over her unsated nakedness and staring at the
brooding figure standing at her bedroom window.

89

'What's on earth's wrong, Dominic?' she asked.
'You wanted me. I know you did.'

He turned to stare at her, at her still avid eyes, and
thought of other dark eyes, eyes which flashed scornfully when they clashed with his, eyes which he
would give anything to have look at him as Shani's
were at that moment.

'It wasn't you I was wanting,' he admitted at last
on a ragged sigh.

'Ahh,' she said knowingly, nodding and reaching
for the packet of cigarettes she kept by the bed.

Smoking after sex was Shani's only vice, health-
wise. She often joked that she liked to keep her two
vices together, lest they both get out of control.

Control was as important to Shani as it was to
Dominic.

He watched as the sheet fell down to her waist,
exposing her bare breasts. She didn't bother to cover
herself again as she pulled herself up against the head-
board. She just sat there smoking, without a conscious
thought of her nakedness.

The memory of Tina agitatedly pulling her top
down over *her* bared breasts popped into his mind.
How she'd hated having exposed herself to him that
way! Her disgust that she'd let him almost seduce her
had been incredibly intense.

Dominic wondered if it was just him she despised,
or all men. That appalling childhood of hers must
have jaundiced her view of the male sex. Sarah's obvious vulnerability to men and sex had certainly
galled her.

Still, she wasn't immune to the pleasures of the
flesh. Obviously she *liked* lovemaking. So it was
probably just him she didn't like.

'Who is she?' Shani asked between puffs.

Dominic snapped out of his see-sawing thoughts. 'Someone I met today.'

'At work?'

'In the office, yes.'

'Client or colleague?'

'Neither.'

'What, then?'

'An angel,' he said.

'An *angel*!' Shani laughed. 'Oh, dear, dear, dear, you *have* got it bad.'

'Not that kind of angel,' he returned ruefully. 'An avenging angel. Straight out of hell. And I'm *not* in love with her.'

'Is that so? Well, if you haven't fallen for her, then why aren't you over here, doing what comes naturally? It's not as though your equipment isn't working.'

Dominic had to confess she was right. He wasn't impotent. Not physically, anyway.

'I simply can't get her out of my mind,' he confessed. 'But it's not love.'

'Love has a way of creeping up on you when you're not looking,' she said, and he frowned at the odd note in her voice.

'My God!' he exclaimed, alarmed. 'Shani... You're not...with me, are you?'

'No, I'm not. Thank heavens. But I was beginning to grow very fond of you, darling. *Too* fond. So it's best we come to an end, I think.'

Dominic didn't know what to say. The thought that Shani was becoming emotionally involved with him was a real shock. Who next?

He made up his mind then and there. He had to

keep away from Tina. Well away. Love was not on his agenda. Not now. Not ever. He wanted his old life back. And his old self. He didn't like being out of control. He didn't like anything that had happened to him today one little bit!

He shot a look at Shani, sitting there, smoking. 'Will you be all right, Shani?' he asked gently.

Her mouth curved into a smile, one of her brassy, confident smiles. 'Perfectly all right, but thank you for asking. Fact is I met this incredibly sexy man the other day whom I fancy something rotten. He fancies me too. Gave me his card. He's a lawyer. Not a tender bone in his body. Unlike you, darling. You really are a big softie at heart, you know that?'

'Me?

You have to be kidding!'

'Actually, no, I'm not.'

He laughed. 'And I thought advertising people were supposed to be good judges of character!'

'Oh, but we are,' Shani said with a perfectly straight face. 'We are.'

Tina groaned at the memory of how she'd let all
that talk with Dominic take a hold of her mind. Even
now her face burned with mortification that she'd
listened to his practised responses so readily.

He'd probably been laughing all the way to the dri...

he'd given it was... She knew why people fantasised

CHAPTER TEN

TINA was sitting at the dressing table in her bedroom,
vigorously brushing her hair. The radio clock on the
bedside table showed eight-thirteen. It was Sunday
night, forty-eight hours since all Tina's misconceptions about sex and herself had been totally blown
apart.

She sighed and stopped the brushing. What an endless weekend it had been!

Initially, she'd been glad when Dominic had
stormed out of the house on their return from Sarah's,
having informed his mother curtly not to expect him
back that weekend.

Any relief, however, had been short-lived. That
night she'd lain awake for hours, thinking of what
Dominic was doing with his girlfriend, tormented
with erotic images and her own insane jealousy.

She'd kept thinking about what he'd said to her,
how he'd been attracted to her from the first moment
he'd seen her, how he'd been aroused all through dinner. She'd felt tortured by the thought it could have
been *her* in his arms that night, not Shani.

No wonder she hadn't slept a wink Friday night!

Tina now knew what Sarah had meant when she'd
tried to explain how she'd felt sometimes when she'd
been with a lover. The mindless madness of it all.
The flights of fantasy which took you out of reality
into a world where nothing existed but your yearning,
burning body with its dark desires and wicked needs.

93

Tina groaned at the memory of how she'd felt on that bed with Dominic. She'd been shameless. Even now her face burned with mortification that she'd fallen victim to his practised expertise so easily.

Still, if nothing else, she now understood the driving power of sex. She saw why people transgressed normal moral boundaries when in the grip of lust. It explained so much about life which had previously confused her.

But all this new knowledge didn't make her own situation any easier to bear. She still lusted after Dominic Hunter like mad—a man she despised. Which, of course, was the main crux of her problem.

If it had been any other man, she could have indulged her feelings without fear of losing too much respect for herself. But how could she succumb to the man who'd seduced Sarah, who'd produced and abandoned Bonnie?

It was an impossible situation, made even more impossible by the fact her normally tough, hard-nosed brain seemed to no longer have any control over her body. Common sense and sheer decency demanded she put aside such a potentially disastrous desire, but she simply couldn't. It obsessed her mind all the time.

During the daytime, she'd managed to get a marginal grip, having things to distract her. Yesterday she'd done the washing in the morning—there was always washing with a baby—and in the afternoon Ida had taken her shopping again.

The dear woman was obviously making up for lost grandmother time by buying Bonnie toys and clothes. Tina hadn't had the heart to tell her not to, that Bonnie already had everything she needed for a while. She already understood full well how a baby like Bonnie, with her unfortunate start in life, could tug at the heartstrings. You just wanted to lavish so much love and attention on her to make up for her losing her mother and not having a father who wanted her.

Today, she and Ida had gone down to the park in the morning, with Bonnie in her pram, then stopped at a local café for a leisurely lunch.

It had been a beautiful spring day, still and sunny without being too hot. After they'd come home, and Bonnie had been bathed, fed and settled for a sleep, Tina had joined Ida picking some roses in the garden. They'd spent a couple of hours arranging them in various vases around the house, during which Tina had kept up a happy face.

But inside she'd still been fretting over her feelings for Dominic Hunter. Every time Ida had brought her son into the conversation—which had been often—Tina had found herself tensing. Of course she hadn't shown it, but it had been a strain, acting all the while.

She'd been rather relieved when Ida had had to go out after dinner. A woman from her bridge club had called, explaining that one of her regular Sunday night players was unwell and they desperately needed a fourth. Could Ida possibly come? She hadn't wanted to at first, but Tina had insisted, thinking it would be good to be alone for a while. Now, she regretted that insistence. Being alone with her thoughts and feelings was *not* such a good idea at all.

Putting the hairbrush down, Tina stood up and walked across the plush cream carpet to the window, which looked down onto the front yard. The driveway was deserted. Tina hoped it would remain that way. The last thing she wanted was Dominic coming home with his mother out. He'd said he wouldn't be home all weekend, which meant that, with a bit of luck, he didn't intend showing up till very late tonight or, even better, Monday morning.

Turning, Tina walked over and into the attached bathroom, which had another door leading into a smaller bedroom where Bonnie was sleeping.

Ida had confessed to Tina when she'd assigned her and Bonnie these rooms that she'd decorated this part of the house, and had this extra door put in, in anticipation of her younger son, Mark, and his wife having children.

Tina had then heard all about Mark, who sounded like an irresponsible dreamer, especially where money was concerned, and nothing like his older brother whom, Ida had explained, had been her financial and emotional rock when her husband had died. A stroke had claimed Dominic's father unexpectedly, seven years earlier. If that hadn't been shock enough for the family, he'd died leaving his business affairs in a right old mess. Overdrawn accounts and second mortgages everywhere!

Dominic had come to the rescue, working crippling hours to get everything back into the black, which was one of the reasons he'd returned to live at home. Firstly because there weren't enough hours in the day for him to look after himself. And secondly because it had saved money on renting elsewhere, his weekly contribution enabling the mortgages on the house to be cleared more quickly.

Of course, everything was fine now, Ida had hastened to explain, perhaps thinking Tina might be worried they weren't in a financial position to help Bonnie. Ida claimed Dominic was as brilliant a financial investor and advisor as his grandfather, who'd apparently made millions in the post-war years, most of which his less skilled son—Dominic's father—had lost, in several speculative and high-risk investments.

Actually, there was no need for Dominic to continue to live at home, Ida had added. She suspected he did it because he thought she'd be lonely without his company.

Tina suspected he did it because he'd discovered it was much easier to have someone else—a woman, naturally—do all the mundane things in life, leaving him free to do the really important things, like make money and seduce women!

Her heart hardening at this thought, Tina tiptoed from the bathroom into the room where Bonnie was sleeping.

Her heart melted as she peered down at the lovely little face. What an incredibly beautiful child she was. Sarah all over again, with perfect skin, long curling eyelashes and the loveliest of mouths. Sweetly shaped, with full lips.

Already you could see she would be a beauty when she grew up. She would need protecting. She would need a father as well as a mother.

'And a father you shall have, my love,' she vowed staunchly.

Making sure Bonnie was firmly tucked in, Tina crept out of the room, leaving the door into the bathroom slightly ajar so that she could hear when Bonnie woke during the night. She was sure to, at least once, having not yet learned to sleep through the night. Ida had said she probably wouldn't till she was on solids, which started around four months. This was confirmed by one of the three books on child-raising Tina

had bought that afternoon while Ida had been looking
at baby clothes.

Once back in her bedroom, a still restless Tina contemplated going downstairs to watch television, but
quickly discarded that idea. She'd already showered
and was wearing her night things.

The prospect of Dominic arriving home and finding
her downstairs attired in skimpy nightwear was foolish in the extreme.

'If you don't want to get burnt,' she warned herself
aloud, 'then stay away from potential fires.'

Being alone with Dominic Hunter would be
a highly flammable situation. Being alone with
Dominic Hunter with nothing covering her sexually
charged body but two thin layers of blue silk would
be inevitable spontaneous combustion.

She didn't have to look down to see that her nipples
were already erect, as they were every time she even
thought of that man in connection with anything re-
motely sexual.

No, there was nothing for it but bed. Thankfully,
she had a novel which she'd taken from one of Ida's
bookshelves and brought up with her earlier. A thriller
which promised to be unputdownable.

She had a feeling she would still be reading it when
Ida arrived home. Around eleven-thirty, she'd said.

Tina had just slipped off her wrap when the sound
of a door slamming downstairs had her scrambling
back into it.

Ida would not have slammed the door that way.
Only a man would do that with a sleeping baby in
the house.

Dominic, it seemed, had finally deigned to come
home.

She heard him call for his mother and receive no reply; heard him hurry up the stairs; heard him prowl along the hallway to his room, then come back again.

Her heart stopped when he halted outside her door, then jumped when he knocked.

'Tina? Are you in there?'

She clasped the brass doorknob with both hands to stop him from turning it. If there'd been a bolt she would have thrown it, but there was no bolt and no key in the lock.

'Yes,' she choked out through the door. 'Why?'

'I can't seem to find Mum.'

He sounded angry. And impatient.

'Your...your mother's out. Playing bridge.'

'But it's not her bridge night!'

'She's standing in for someone.'

'For pity's sake, open the damned door and talk to me properly,' he snapped. 'I can hardly hear you.'

'I can't. I...I'm not dressed.'

'At *this* hour of the night? Since when do grown women go to bed before eight-thirty?'

'Since they started getting up in the middle of the night to look after babies!' she snapped back. 'Now go away and leave me alone.'

He hesitated, then went, the wooden floorboards protesting as he clomped his way down the upstairs hallway back in the direction of his rooms. A door banged shut, shortly after which the water pipes registered the whooshing sound of someone having a shower.

When Tina finally let go of the doorknob her knees went to jelly. So close, she thought shakily, and stumbled over to the bed. Once there, she fell in, then just lay there, a tremor claiming her every now and then.

She felt weak as a kitten, and strangely bereft. Tears filled her eyes. Angry with herself, she blinked them away and pulled the bedclothes over her.

'I will not cry over that man,' she resolved, and determinedly picked up the novel.

Tina was still on page one several minutes later when the water pipes fell silent. Once again she found herself tensing and listening for him. She was just about to relax and return to reading when the sound of a door opening and shutting put her nerve-endings on red alert once more.

He was walking along the hallway back towards her door again, moving closer and closer. The fact that he had to pass her room to go downstairs did come to mind, but was instantly dismissed. He wasn't going to go past. She just knew it.

And she was right. His footsteps stopped outside her room. She could almost hear him breathing, which was crazy since the door was one of the old-fashioned kind. Solid wood and thick. Not the sort of door you could hear things through easily. Certainly not mere breathing.

The abrupt knocking tightened her nerves further.

'Tina?' he called through the door, his voice a low growl.

She didn't answer, her breath frozen in her lungs. At the same time her heart was hammering behind her ribs and some simply dreadful part of her wanted him to walk right in without asking.

'Your light's still on,' he ground out.

'I...I'm reading,' she croaked.

'We have to talk, Tina.'

'No, we don't,' she countered, panic in her voice and in her heart.

'I have things I have to say to you.'

'Tell me in the morning.'

'No. I need to say them now, or I won't sleep.'

When Tina saw the doorknob turn, she squawked and dived out of the bed, colliding forcibly with Dominic's big broad chest as he came in. Her hands flew up in a defenceless gesture, only to encounter a deep V of bare chest, along with a surprisingly soft triangle of black curls.

'Oh!' she cried, her flustered eyes finally focusing on this provocative expanse of naked flesh before flicking agitatedly down, then up again.

He was wearing long black silk pyjama bottoms, with a matching dressing-gown sashed inadequately around his impressive body. His feet were bare, the skin under her hands cool and faintly damp.

Tina tried not to stare, or to feel, but that was all she seemed to be able to do at that moment.

Stare...and feel.

Her eyes would not obey her mental commands. As for her hands...they were frozen flat on his flesh, but her sensitive fingertips were registering—and revelling in—the feel of all that macho maleness beneath them.

Her head fairly spun with desire.

Suddenly, his size didn't intimidate her at all. She found it tantalising. And irresistible. She ached to touch him all over, to discover all that made him the man he was.

It was like being possessed, she realised dazedly as her eyes lifted inexorably to his. Someone else was inhabiting her body, some reckless and very foolish female who was about to ignore the fact that this was the last man on earth she should let seduce her.

Her brain screamed at her that it wasn't too late to stop.

But her brain was powerless against the commands of her suddenly awakened sexuality, with all its urgent desires and needy, greedy demands.

CHAPTER ELEVEN

DOMINIC only wanted to tell Tina he'd found out who Bonnie's real father was. Damn it all, he'd spent all weekend finding out!

He'd raced home, anxious to tell both his mother and Tina the truth, and put an end to this farce. He'd even planned to generously offer a sum of money to Tina for the child, so his stupid conscience wouldn't bother him afterwards.

He'd arrived home, desperate to have done with it all before he went to bed and tried to get a decent night's sleep for the first time since Friday. And what had happened? His mother was out and Tina wouldn't talk to him.

Who could blame him for insisting? A man could only take so much.

And now look where his impatience had got him! In a bedroom with a scantily clad Tina. Hell, a near *naked* Tina, who was looking up at him in a way he'd thought she'd *never* look at him. Worse, she was actually touching him, her palms hot against the treacherous flesh he'd so desperately tried to calm and control under a long cold shower.

For a few seconds he tried to struggle out from under the white-hot haze of desire which had instantly clouded his mind. But it was hard when she was so darned desirable-looking. That glorious black hair tumbled wildly over her bare shoulders. The hardened nipples outlined in pale blue silk. The wide, sensual mouth already parted in the most provocative way.

What was he to do? Stop and try to work out what was going on here? Complain that she was the most contradictory, infuriating woman in the world? Refuse to touch her till she listened and agreed he wasn't the rat she thought he was?

With any other woman Dominic might have managed any of those courses of action. Easily. With *this* woman, however, he could not wait, or think straight. He had to touch her back right then and there, had to make love to her. *Had* to.

These compulsive feelings were not accepted happily by Dominic. He still didn't like his lack of control where Tina was concerned. Or the confusion she evoked in him. Even as he surrendered to the inevitable, he felt angry with himself.

And her.

Tina saw his eyes darken, then narrow. She knew what he was going to do. She didn't need to be told.

The knowledge electrified her.

Yes, kiss me, she willed with a wild, wanton recklessness. *Kiss me. Touch me. Do anything you want with me.*

Kicking the door shut behind him, he grasped her wrists in a less than gentle grip and wound them around behind her back, pulling downwards till her back arched almost painfully. She gasped, then watched, open-mouthed, as his head bent, not to her lips but to one of her silk-encased breasts.

His lips parted and closed over the already erect peak, sucking on it, drawing it in deep before abruptly letting it go. By then the silk was soaked and the nipple throbbing. When he began licking and nibbling at it, Tina made mewing little sounds of pleasure.

His head jerked up and he glowered down at her, a wild man with wild eyes. He let her wrists go and yanked the straps of the nightie off her shoulders, tugging it downwards till it pooled at her feet.

She straightened and just stood there, naked, dazed.

He stared at her for a long moment, before stripping himself just as quickly, Tina only having a brief glimpse of his impressive body before he scooped her up and carried her over to the bed, falling with her into its cool, downy depths.

And then they were kissing and clawing at each other, tongues tangling, limbs entwining, hands frantically exploring. He groaned when her fingers brushed over the tip of his penis, then moaned when she returned to stroke the full length of him.

He growled some kind of protest and took her wrists once more, locking them up above her head within a single iron grip. His other hand spread her legs, then zeroed in on what lay between them.

Tina had never known anything as exciting, or as electric. Her head whipped from side to side between her captured arms, her heart racing like an express train. Sensation built upon sensation as those merciless fingers explored and probed, tantalised and tormented.

'Please, oh, please,' she whimpered, her body desperately wanting more, wanting *him*, not his hands. Her legs moved wider apart in the most wanton invitation.

And then he was there, thrusting into her emptiness, satisfying her need to be filled, and fulfilled.

Tina gasped at the force and power of his possession, then groaned when he began to move. Inspired by sheer instinct, she moved with him, meeting each forward surge with an upward lift of her hips. Heat built up in her body and she was panting as if she'd run up a thousand steps. A pressure was forming within her, a tightness gripping her chest. Her head was spinning and the air became thick and heavy.

Tina was just thinking she might have a heart attack when suddenly something seemed to shatter inside her. Great grasping spasms came in waves, bringing with them flashes of blinding pleasure.

Groaning, she clutched at a pillow and squeezed her eyes tightly shut. But his tortured cry sent them flying open again and she watched, her own chest heaving, while Dominic came, his back arching, his mouth grimacing in a mixture of agony and ecstasy. She felt his flesh pumping deep within her, felt the flood of heat, felt a satisfaction so deep that she feared nothing would stop her from wanting to experience this again and again and again.

It was a very sobering thought.

This was what had turned Sarah into a fool, she realised with a bitter dismay. This was what would turn *her* into a fool, she conceded.

If she let it.

If she let him.

Dominic collapsed across her, exhausted. For a few moments he could not help but wallow in the sheer pleasure of it all, because nothing in his sexual experience could match what he and Tina had just shared.

The moment he'd surged into her for the first time would live in his mind for ever. The mad mixture of

erotic rapture and dark triumph. The glorious feel of
his naked flesh fusing with hers. And then the actual
climax itself, releasing him finally from the physical
and emotional tension which had been building up in
him since Friday.

But any wallowing swiftly came to an end as reality intervened. Because, of course, he hadn't used a
condom. He'd thought of it briefly at one stage, but
had swiftly pushed the impulse aside. He'd been too
desperate to make love, too much out of control to
stop.

Dear God. What a mess he'd made of his vow to
avoid Tina at all costs!

Slowly, he levered himself up onto his elbows and
looked down at her. When she looked back up at him
with coldly contemptuous eyes he shuddered inside.

'Glad to see you always use protection,' she bit out.

Dominic sighed, realising his credibility had just
been shattered. Whatever he had to say about Sarah's
mystery boyfriend would be water off a duck's back
now. Even worse was the possibility that, this time,
he *might* have conceived an unwanted child.

His life since he'd met Tina, he realised wearily,
was becoming very complicated indeed.

'Is that going to be a big problem?' he forced himself to ask in a reasonably calm voice.

'Fortunately…no.'

He could not disguise his relief. 'Thank God.
You're on the pill, I presume?'

She gave him another long, cold look. 'That's
right,' she snapped, then added tartly, 'Unlike poor
Sarah.'

Dominic eyed her sharply, about to say something
in his defence, then decided, Why bother? That par-

ticular problem would sort itself out when the DNA test came back. Then and only then would he tell her the truth as he saw it. Any earlier and he would just be wasting his breath.

Meanwhile, what was he going to do about what had just happened?

'We really do need to talk now, Tina,' he said in all seriousness.

'No, we don't,' she retorted, and rolled out from under him, ejecting him from her body so abruptly that he gasped in pain. He watched, stunned, while she snatched up a blue satin robe from the end of the bed and slid into it, wrapping it tightly around her naked body before looking at him again.

'What's to talk about?' she threw at him defiantly while her dark eyes glittered and flashed. 'So we had sex? Big deal. You wanted it. I wanted it. We had it. End of story.'

Dominic was shocked how much her attitude hurt. If Shani had said the same thing, he would not have felt offended. He would have laughed.

Instead, a fierce resentment fired his blood.

How dared she reduce what they had just shared to nothing but sex? It might not have been love, but it had been more than two animals mindlessly mating. There was something emotional at work here, something complex and very, very human.

'Don't talk such rubbish!' he snapped. 'If that was your attitude then you would have let me have sex with you on Sarah's bed last Friday night. Because you wanted it then, all right, as well. Instead, you stopped me. And rightly so. That would have been in very poor taste.'

'And you think it's not very poor taste for you to

sleep with me after spending the weekend in another woman's bed?' she countered savagely.

'I did no such thing,' he grated out. 'I went to Shani's flat on Friday night but I left without sleeping with her. In fact, Shani and I have agreed to call it quits. I spent the weekend at a hotel. I found I couldn't go to bed with another woman when it was you I wanted. Only you, Tina.'

For a split second he saw something wonderful in her eyes. They lit up with amazement and pleasure and…

But then the light died, replaced by an implacable coldness. 'I'm sorry, Dominic,' she said in chilling tones, 'but I don't believe you. Just as I don't believe you used a condom with Sarah. I can only hope and pray you don't make a habit of unsafe sex. Now I'm going to the bathroom, if you don't mind.'

He lay there on the rumpled bed, broodily waiting for her return, furious with her ongoing poor opinion of him. As the minutes ticked away he was seriously tempted to reveal the facts he'd learned over the weekend, even though he had no proof of what he'd been told. It was only hearsay.

Still, if he could convince Tina he *might* not be Bonnie's father, and that Sarah *hadn't* come to him asking for help, then maybe…well, maybe…

Well, maybe *what*, you jerk? the voice of male reason demanded testily. Surely you don't want to go anywhere with this, do you?

Serious self-irritation was beginning to set him.

When Dominic heard the shower running at full bore, a different irritation surfaced to scrape over his already raw ego. She just couldn't wait to wash him from her body, could she? As if he'd made her dirty or something.

There'd been nothing dirty done here tonight in his opinion. It had been one darned special experience for both of them, and the sooner she recognised that the better! The sooner she recognised he wasn't the womanising rat she thought he was the better too!

She was ages in the bathroom, even after the shower had been turned off—so long, in fact, that he almost jumped up and banged on the door.

He was about to do so when the door opened and she came in looking upset, the baby in her arms.

'I woke her up with the shower,' she explained, her face flushed. 'I didn't think. I'll have to go and get her a bottle now. Do you think you could mind her for a minute while I run downstairs?'

Recalling the last time she'd handed him the baby, Dominic experienced a brief moment of panic, but hid it well, hoping to redeem himself a little in Tina's eyes.

'Sure,' he said breezily, and hauled himself up into a sitting position in the bed, popping a couple of pillows behind his back. 'Bring her over here.'

'Could you put some clothes on first, please?' she said, glaring at him.

He doubted a three-month-old baby would have minded his nudity, but thought it best not to point that out.

Diving out of the bed, he retrieved his pyjama bottoms from the floor and dragged them on. Her sense of modesty hopefully satisfied, Dominic returned to his position on the bed before looking her way.

'Ready,' he said.

She glowered at the amount of bare chest still

showing, but didn't say anything, merely sighed, walked over and handed him the baby. 'I'll try not to be too long,' she said. 'If she cries, then rock her, or walk her up and down and sing to her.'

'Right,' he said softly, remembering how the last time his deep voice had frightened the child. With a bit of luck, none of those things would be required, especially the singing bit. He was so tone deaf that he'd been offered bribes by his classmates *not* to sing at school concerts.

As luck would have it, no sooner had Tina departed than the baby took one look at the big male face peering down at her and began to bawl. Dominic was not only walking in a flash, but rocking at the same time. That worked for a few seconds, till the little pink terror realised *who* it was doing the walking and rocking and let rip again.

'No way I'm going to sing too,' he told the crying but tearless infant. 'I'm not much good at telling fairy stories either. They always say to talk about what you know, so here goes...' And he launched into a description of his job.

Dominic paused to draw breath a couple of minutes later, only then realising that the baby's pretty pink mouth had stopped squawking. In fact her baby blue eyes were fixed on his in rapt attention, almost as though she'd been listening to every word he said, and was holding her breath waiting for more.

'Well, blow me down,' he whispered under his breath. 'She likes hearing about business. Oh, what a smart girl you are,' he crooned, relieved at having found a way to stop that nerve-scraping noise.

'Now, the stockmarket is like a big international sports arena,' he explained as he settled them both back on the bed, 'where this very complex game is being played twenty-four hours a day, with thousands of different rules and pitfalls. But, oh, what fun once you master those rules and avoid those pitfalls. There's nothing else like it in the world! Still, you have a lot to learn if you're going to grow up and play *that* particular game, my girl. Now...where shall I begin?'

CHAPTER TWELVE

TINA heard Bonnie start to cry just as she reached the bottom of the stairs, but she kept on going, her need to be away from that man far greater than any worry about the baby.

A little crying wasn't going to kill Bonnie. But staying in the same room as Dominic Hunter might just result in Tina killing *him*!

Oh, the smugness of the man! The arrogance! And the insensitivity!

Couldn't he appreciate how she must feel, having gone to bed with *him*, of all men? Couldn't he understand how this had to be affecting her pride, and her self-respect?

Of course not, she realised angrily. Men like him didn't think about a woman's pride or self-respect. Women were just sex-objects to be toyed with, lied to, then discarded.

What gall he had to claim he hadn't been to bed with his girlfriend that weekend, that he'd broken up with this Shani because of *her*.

Yeah, right! And the tooth fairy got engaged to Santa Claus this weekend as well!

And then there was the matter of his not using protection, something he'd claimed he never, ever did. Okay, so maybe he *did* use a condom most of the time. He struck Tina as a normally intelligent and pragmatic individual who wouldn't make a habit of sexual stupidity. But tonight proved his flesh could be as weak as the next man's.

Tina wondered what would have happened if she'd told him she *wasn't* on the pill at all. Which she wasn't. It might have almost been worth it just to see the look on his face!

Actually, she hadn't lied about that for *his* benefit but for her own. She hadn't wanted to explain that you could set a clock by her cycle, that she knew her body like the back of her hand and that she was positive she'd ovulated over a week ago. If she were a betting person, she'd put a billion dollars on her period arriving around midday the following Saturday.

No, there would be no baby from what had transpired up in that bedroom tonight. Thank God. Still, Tina found the thought appalling that if she'd met Dominic a week ago, right around the wrong time, she would still have gone to bed with him. She wouldn't have given conception a moment's thought, till *after* the event.

Which brought her to the other reason she'd lied to him about being on the pill. She wanted him to think she was sexually active. No way did she want him finding out it had been a couple of years since her last sexual encounter, or that she'd only ever had two very brief and unsuccessful affairs in her whole life. She wanted him to believe her claim that it had just been sex between them, and that he wasn't anything special to her.

Because he darned well wasn't!

He was just an…an…aberration. A perverse infatuation. For some weird and wonderful reason unbeknown to her, he turned her on in a big, big way. Now more than ever. She'd hardly been able to look

at him in that bedroom a minute ago without wanting
to touch him again. If only he'd put on the black silk
dressing-gown as well, instead of just the pyjama bottoms. He'd left far too much exposed flesh for her
needy, greedy gaze. She'd ached to run her hands
over that magnificent chest again.

Tina groaned as desire contracted her own stomach
once more. Oh, why had she brought the baby in to
him like that? Why?

She'd thought she was using Bonnie as some kind
of protection, to guard her from these dark desires.
Instead, she now knew to her shame that nothing was
going to protect her from this ungovernable lust. She
would just have to endure it as best she could. *Hide*
it as best she could.

Men like him enjoyed having power over women.
They probably revelled in being adored, and fawned
over, and *loved*. In hindsight, she recalled a trium-
phant glint in his eyes when he'd had her spreadea-
gled before him. He'd liked it when she'd begged,
then become annoyed when she'd left the bed so
abruptly afterwards.

Well, she wouldn't beg the next time.

Tina sucked in a sharp breath. The next time. She
was already thinking of the *next* time. Dear Lord,
what was happening to her?

With a shaking hand she picked the bottle out of
the simmering water and tested the temperature on
her wrist. Warm enough, she decided. Time to go
upstairs, sweep Bonnie out of Dominic's too tempting
arms and escape into the sanctuary of the baby's
room.

With the bottle in hand, she was hurrying up the
stairs when the surprise of silence upstairs slowed her

step. Frowning, she listened, but there was no baby crying at all.

Once she reached the top landing, however, she could hear voices coming through the slightly ajar doorway. No, not voices, she soon realised. One voice. Dominic's, talking with expression, as though he were reading Bonnie a story.

She drew closer and listened, her eyes widening as she heard the content of that story. Not *The Three Bears*. Or *Red Riding-Hood*. Or *Jack and the Beanstalk*. He was telling Bonnie all about stocks and shares!

Amazed, Tina peeped in through the gap in the doorway and blinked at the scene before her eyes. Dominic was sitting back against the bedhead with his knees bent and Bonnie lying against his silk-encased thighs. He was holding both her hands out wide and regaling her with what signs to look for in a bull market, as opposed to a bear market.

Bonnie was staring up at him as though he were one of the gods on Mount Olympus.

Exasperation battled with the sudden awful temptation to be charmed by the scene.

Exasperation won. How like Sarah's daughter to be so easily captivated by a man!

Letting out an irritable sigh, Tina pushed open the door and stalked in, halting by the bed to glare down at him. Dominic simply ignored her while he finished educating his daughter about the various stockmarket crashes over the years.

Fury sent an impatient hand to her hip and a combative glint to her eyes.

'The smarties always read the signs and get out before the rot sets in,' Dominic was advising. 'I'd tell you all those signs in detail, but your mummy's here with your bottle. We'll have to leave the rest of this till later, sweetie.'

Dominic's calling her 'mummy' and Bonnie 'sweetie' like that caused Tina's stomach to curl over and her heart to go to mush. As did the sight of him very gently scooping Bonnie up from his thighs and placing her so carefully in the crook of his left arm. 'I'll feed her if you like,' he offered, and held out his right hand for the bottle. 'Give you a break.'

Tina swallowed, then rather reluctantly gave it to him. As much as it was her dream for Dominic to accept and bond with his child, how could she continue to hate him when face to face with such tenderness?

She watched him angle the bottle into the baby's eager mouth, noting the startled pleasure in his face when Bonnie's tiny hand came up to cover his, as was her habit with anyone who fed her. Tina remembered how she'd felt the first time Bonnie had done it to her, the innocently trusting gesture tugging at her till then hard heart, sparking the beginning of her new and amazing maternal feelings. Was her father feeling something similar? Had the first seed of love just been sown?

Dominic looked up suddenly, his expression pained. 'You know, Tina, I would never deny being Bonnie's father if I thought I really *was* her father. You must believe me on this.'

For the first time real doubt seeped in, and Tina felt sick.

Dominic looked back down at Bonnie but kept on speaking, his voice low and reasoned. 'I think I know

who her father is. I spent a great deal of time over
the weekend finding out.'

'You did?' she echoed faintly.

He glanced up again. 'Yes. I told you. I wasn't with
Shani. Good Lord, what does it take to have you believe me for once? Think, woman! What motive could
I possibly have to lie? I've agreed to have the DNA
test tomorrow, but I already know what the result will
be. I know you think tonight proves I'm sexually irresponsible, but I swear to you, Tina, that tonight was
the first time in twelve years that I've had unsafe sex.
I'm fanatical about it, usually.'

Tina was inclined to believe him. About the condom, anyway.

'Tonight was a first for me too,' she confessed. 'For
unsafe sex, that is.'

'I think tonight was a first for both of us in lots of
ways, don't you?' he said softly.

'What…what do you mean?'

'I mean it was something very special, Tina. Something unique. I don't know about you but I know I've
never felt for another woman what I've been feeling
since I met you. To be honest, it's rattled the hell out
of me. I like to live an ordered life. I like to be in
control. Falling madly in love is not on my agenda.
But I'm not one to—'

'It's not love,' she broke in firmly, frightened over
where this was going. 'It's just lust.'

'You sound pretty sure of that.'

'I'm very sure. I've been there, done that. Lots of
times.'

He looked taken aback. 'You're saying tonight
wasn't anything special for you? That you've felt this
kind of passion before?'

'It's always pretty exciting the first time.'

He just stared at her, and she felt worse than she'd ever felt in her life. Chilled, and ashamed.

He swung his feet over the side of the bed, stood up, and handed Bonnie back to her. 'You can finish this. I'm wasting my time here, with both of you.'

'But aren't you going to tell me what you found out?' she asked.

His eyes stabbed disgust at her. 'What's the point? I have no real proof of my findings, only hearsay. You already have much more hearsay evidence against me. Not to mention that other mysterious evidence you won't show me. I only hope that by the time the DNA test comes back my mother isn't too attached to that sweet little child, because Mum doesn't deserve to be hurt. She's endured enough emotional pain in her life. Maybe you should give that some thought when you're lying in your bed tonight, all alone with your prejudices and your hypocrisies. Oh, and I sure hope you enjoyed your first time with me, honey, because it was your first and last!'

Scooping up his robe from the floor, he stormed out of the room, banging the door shut behind him so loudly that Bonnie spat out the bottle and started crying.

It's always pretty exciting the first time.'

CHAPTER THIRTEEN

DOMINIC muttered into his beard as he clomped down the hallway and into his bedroom, slamming that door for good measure as well. He'd never been a door-slammer till he'd met Miss Tina Ballbreaker Highsmith, but he rather imagined he would get very good at it by the time she left his abode.

"It's always pretty exciting the first time," he mimicked aloud in that dismissive fashion she specialised in, and which set his teeth on edge at the best of times. This time, however, she'd cut him to the quick.

Okay, so she'd probably had great sex hundreds of times. Well, so had he! But this hadn't been just great sex. It had been a great *experience*. A combination of the emotional and the physical. Or it had been for him.

Clearly she didn't have enough sensitivity to know the damned difference!

He paced angrily around the large room, calling her all sorts of uncomplimentary names, working his way through the alphabet. When he came to witch and whore, he couldn't think of any more and sank down wearily onto the side of the bed.

No point in trying to sleep, he knew.

Dominic rose and walked over to turn on the computer he kept at home.

'Might as well work,' he muttered, and sat down.

But his mind kept wandering, first back to Tina,

then to the bed behind him, then idly around the room.

It had once been the master bedroom, but after his father had died and he'd come back home to live his mother had insisted he have it. After much argument, he'd agreed.

Admittedly, it was the only bedroom in the house which had enough space for a small home office, along with other normal bedroom-type furniture. But the thought of sleeping in his parents' bed had made him cringe at first. He'd overheard far too many arguments over what had transpired there, or *not* transpired there. He knew personally of one young lady in his father's employ—a cleaner—whom the master of the house had regularly bonked on the marital mattress.

Lord knows how many others there had been!

So, with his mother's permission, Dominic had donated her old bedroom suite to charity and bought himself a nice large new bed, after which he'd brought in the carpenters.

Now, one wall carried built-in storage for his clothes and personal effects while another housed a compact home office, the PC linked to the computers at work. His own television and video remained hidden behind a cupboard, the wall of which slid back at the touch of a switch.

Not that he used them much. But they were there, when needed.

His mother's bedroom was now downstairs, in what had once been his father's study. She rarely had to trudge up and down the stairs these days, which was a lot easier on her varicose veins. Dominic paid for a cleaner to come in every Monday and Friday to do all the heavy housework, along with the laundry. He also paid for the cook, June, who came in most afternoons for a few hours. Money well spent, in his opinion. His mother was the most appalling cook. Other than that, he had a chap pop round once a fortnight to mow the lawns and trim the edges, as well as occasionally dig up a garden bed. His mother did most of the gardening. It was her pride and joy, as well as her hobby.

Thinking about his mother turned his mind back to what he'd found out this past weekend. Sheer stubbornness now prevented his telling Tina, but he really had to tell his mother. So he went downstairs, poured himself a hefty glass of port and settled in front of the television to await her arrival home.

He heard her key in the door just as the Sunday night movie's credits went up, shortly after eleven.

He stayed where he was, knowing full well she would pop her head in to see who was still up.

'Oh, it's you,' she said shortly afterwards, in the sort of tone he might have expected from Tina.

Clearly he was still not the flavour of the month.

'Yes, it's me,' he returned drily from where he remained seated in his favourite armchair. 'Your loving son.'

'Where's Tina? I suppose you've bullied her into her room with your presence?'

'Yep, that's me as well,' he drawled. 'Bully-boy. Not to mention callous seducer and abandoner of pregnant women. So, yes, Tina has retired, but only after I'd dragged her up there by the hair on her head and had my wicked way with her.'

His mother sighed. 'You've argued again.'

He half smiled. If only she knew. 'You could say that,' he murmured.

'What about *this* time?'

'Let's just say Tina and I couldn't agree if our lives depended on it.'

'Bonnie's asleep?'

'I imagine so. Everything's certainly quiet on the upstairs front.'

'I think I'll go to bed too, then. I'm tired.'

'Before you do, Mum, there's something I have to tell you.'

She hesitated in the doorway, her glance rueful. 'It's a little late to confess all, don't you think? I already know you're Bonnie's father.'

'That's just it, Mum. I'm not. Damien Parsons is. I did some investigating over the weekend and Sarah had been having an affair with him.'

'Oh, Dominic, Dominic,' Ida said sadly, shaking her head at him. 'Putting the blame on a dead man is such a shoddy thing to do.'

Dominic could not believe his ears. What was wrong with these women? 'But, Mum, Sarah *slept* with him! I know it for a fact.'

'And she slept with you too, didn't she? Bonnie is *your* child, son. Believe me on this.'

'But she doesn't even *look* like me.'

'Don't be ridiculous!' she countered impatiently. 'Of course she does. It's just that she's a girl and you're blind to the resemblances.'

Dominic rolled his eyes. This was hopeless. He rose from the chair and walked over to his mother, placing a caring hand on her shoulder.

'Mum,' he said softly, 'I just don't want you to get hurt.'

Her expression was genuinely bewildered. 'But how can I get hurt? Tina's a lovely, generous-hearted girl. She *wants* me to be a part of Bonnie's life. She wants *you* to be a part of Bonnie's life too.'

'Mum, for pity's sake, will you *listen* to me?'

He looked at her imploringly, but could see by her eyes that she'd already clicked off to that subject. 'You know,' she said, shaking her head, 'when I first saw Tina I thought to myself she was just your type of girl. You always did go for feisty females. And most women seem to go for you, though to be honest I'm not sure why. Oh, you're good-looking enough, I suppose. And you've been blessed with a great body. But you don't go to any trouble to attract them. I guess it was hoping for too much to think you two might hit it off and get married.'

'Married!' he exclaimed. 'Good God, has everyone in this house gone insane?'

'Everyone? Who else are you talking about?'

'Me, Mum,' he muttered, and brushed past her to march back upstairs. *'Me!'*

CHAPTER FOURTEEN

'AREN'T you feeling well, Tina?' Ida asked as they came out of the doctor's surgery. Dominic had just stalked off in the direction of the car park, Tina sighing with relief at his departure.

Breakfast had been a nightmare. And so had sitting in the waiting room together till they'd been called in to the surgery.

Dominic hadn't said a word all morning, not even during the process of the nurse taking his blood, or Bonnie's, only afterwards brusquely asking the doctor to see if he could hurry up the pathologist with the results, to which the doctor had said he'd do his best, but he doubted they'd get them in under two weeks. Tina had seen Dominic's mouth thin at this, and knew he was having as hard a time as she was.

'No, I'm fine,' she lied to Ida. 'I'm just a little tense this morning. I was worried Bonnie might get upset at the needle.'

'That's understandable. But she only cried for a minute. Look,' she said, nodding down at the pram, 'she's gone back to sleep already.'

'Yes. She's such a good little baby. Such a good little sleeper.'

'You look like *you* could do with a sleep.'

'Yes,' she admitted wearily. 'I didn't get much last night.'

'And I know why!' Ida pronounced. 'Dominic told me.'

Tina froze, then stared at Dominic's mother. 'He told you...what?' she managed to get out.

'That you'd argued again last night.'

'Oh. Oh, yes. Yes, I'm afraid we did.'

'I can understand how annoyed you must be over that Damien Parsons business.'

'Damien Parsons?' she echoed blankly.

'The man Dominic is claiming Sarah had an affair with. He was the head accountant for Hunter & Associates. Married, of course. Not that that stopped Damien from sleeping around. He was always a one for the ladies. An extremely good-looking man. And as suave as they come.'

Tina frowned. He sounded just like the type Sarah would have fallen for. Now *why* did that name Parsons ring a bell?

'Poor Joanna,' Ida murmured, and the penny dropped for Tina. Damien Parsons must be married to Joanna Parsons, the woman Ida had put off coming to dinner the other night. Tina gnawed at her bottom lip while she bounced possibilities back and forth in her mind. This Damien's being a married man could explain Sarah not wanting to reveal his identity and perhaps using Dominic as the perfect patsy when Tina had mercilessly grilled her friend over her new lover.

Tina frowned, then frowned some more when another thought hit. 'You said Joanna was a widow, didn't you?' she asked Ida.

'Yes, Damien was killed in a car accident earlier this year. His own fault. He'd been drinking and driving. Lost control on a wet road and skidded into a telegraph pole.'

Tina was mulling all this information over in her

head when she suddenly realised something else. Damien's name began with a D.

All the blood drained from Tina's face. Oh, dear God...what have I done?

'But none of this matters, you know,' Ida was rattling on. 'I told Dominic straight. Little Bonnie is *your* child, I said. It's useless pointing the finger elsewhere. Face up to fatherhood like a man.'

A clamminess claimed Tina which wasn't the humidity. 'I...I think I'd better sit down,' she said, and sank onto a low cement wall which ran along the side of the pavement.

'Oh, dearie me,' Ida fussed. 'You've gone as white as a sheet. Look, I think we should get you over to my car and into some air-conditioning. It's rather hot out here. Here, lean on the pram. Then, after we get home, I think you should have a lie-down. I'll mind Bonnie. We can bring her bassinette downstairs for the day while you get a good sleep. That way, if she cries, she won't wake you.'

'You're very kind,' Tina said weakly, tears awfully close. What was it Dominic had said to her? He didn't want his mother hurt. She'd been through enough in her life.

Tina supposed he'd been referring to his mother losing her husband as a relatively young woman, then that married son of hers deserting his wife to become a monk. And now *she'd* come along and foolishly raised the poor woman's hopes over the grandchild she'd always wanted.

Tina felt awful. Simply awful!

Dominic paced up and down his office.

He felt awful. Simply awful!

What a pig he'd been this morning: giving every-one the cold shoulder; acting like a sulky child; clomping out of the surgery without a word even to his mother. No wonder she'd looked at him with such disappointment in her eyes.

As for Tina. She'd seemed to have had the stuffing knocked out of her this morning. There hadn't been a hint of the girl who'd bulldozed herself into his life last week, spitting fire and vengeance at him. She'd looked pale and fragile, with dark circles under her eyes and a depressed slump in her normally assertive shoulders.

It had come to him during the slow drive across the bridge and into the city that maybe she'd been protecting herself last night by adopting that good-time-girl attitude. Maybe she'd been acting a part. She was an actress after all.

Given her antagonism towards him, their out-of-control, out-of-this-world lovemaking must have come as a shock. The blushing girl who'd agitatedly pulled down her top last Friday night could not possibly be the hard-nosed promiscuous piece she'd portrayed herself as afterwards.

Maybe she'd bolted out of that bed because she'd been afraid to stay with him. Afraid of what she might say and feel and do.

It hadn't just been sex for her, Dominic had finally concluded, just as he was reaching the toll gates on the bridge. It had been anything but!

He'd almost driven right through the gate without paying at that point, braking savagely at the last second. The collector had given him a narrow-eyed glare, and Dominic had wondered if he'd recognised him from his crossing the other night when Tina had been sitting in the passenger seat, weeping.

This thought had swiftly wiped away any ecstatic joy Dominic had been feeling, an agonised guilt taking over. By the time he'd closed his office door behind him he'd been sweating with the reality he would never be able to make it right with Tina.

She had every reason to hate him, he accepted now as he paced up and down. He'd been brutal to her from the start. First he'd had her forcibly thrown out of this building. Then he'd accused her of being a con-artist. He'd been rude and hostile and downright difficult.

To top it all off, when he'd been besieged with what he'd seen as nothing more than an inconvenient lust, he'd taken advantage of her when she'd been vulnerable and upset. Then, last night, once he'd realised the chemistry was mutual, he'd really gone for the jugular, making love to her like a man possessed, without even protecting her.

No wonder she'd been desperate to protect herself afterwards, to keep him at a safe distance. She had to have been shell-shocked.

And now she was lost to him. Hell, in two weeks' time, she would be irretrievably lost to him. The DNA test would come back and she would be gone from his life. For ever.

Unless…

Dominic sat down at his desk and put his mind to coming up with a plan of action.

Once he did, the ruthless daring of his idea took his breath away. But he only had two weeks at best, and he couldn't let her go, could he? Not now that he'd found the woman his mother had always said he'd one day meet, not now he'd actually fallen in love!

Tina tossed and turned on top of the bed. She could not sleep. It was useless. Her mind went round and round. As tired as she was, she simply could not lie there and do nothing. She had to go to Dominic; to talk to him; apologise; explain.

She knew he must hate her now, but she wasn't thinking of herself so much but his mother, and Bonnie.

A sob caught in her throat. Poor little Bonnie. No father to love her. And probably no grandparents, either. Even if this Damien's parents were alive, would they accept the child of their dead son's bit on the side? Tina doubted it. Besides, what right had she to upset them further in their grief, spoiling their son's reputation and their memory of him?

And what of Ida's friend, Joanna, Damien's widow? Did she deserve to have someone come along and claim her husband had an illegitimate child?

Tina could not imagine any woman wanting to know about her dead husband's baby by another woman.

No, Tina decided. She could not do it, could not barge into another family's life and cause the havoc she'd caused here. She no longer had the stomach for it. Or the will.

Which meant she would have to raise Bonnie all by herself, with no financial or emotional help.

Tina swung her legs over the side of the bed and stood up, squaring her shoulders. She could do it. She could do anything.

But first she had to go and see Dominic and try to put things right.

Dominic was making a list of how he could get around the problem of the DNA results when the telephone rang. He lifted the receiver and said, 'Yes, Doris,' just as he printed, *'IF ALL ELSE FAILS, BRIBE THE PATHOLOGIST'* against tactic number three.

Number one was to win Tina's love and trust so he could happily ring the doctor and cancel the test altogether. Number two was to instruct the doctor to send the results to him first, where he would feed the page—or pages—into his computer, change the results and print out a new report.

'I have a young lady here who wants to see you, Mr Hunter,' Doris whispered in a conspiratorial voice. 'It's *her*.'

'Her?'

'The same one as last Friday. The one with the baby. Only this time the baby's not with her. Do you want me to call Security to throw her out again?'

Dominic dropped his pen. 'Good grief, no, Doris. Don't do that!'

'But, Mr Hunter, on Friday you said I was to call Security if she so much as walked past the door!'

He shook his head. Was it only Friday when that had happened? Only three days ago?

It felt like a lifetime!

'I made a mistake, Doris. She's not who I thought she was. And that gorgeous baby *is* mine, as it turns out. I'll be right out.'

* * *

Tina watched the secretary's eyes grow round, then stare up at her.

Tina groaned. 'He's not going to have me thrown out again, is he?' The woman had cupped the phone so that Tina couldn't hear what had been said, though the word 'security' had filtered through.

Dominic's secretary was still sitting there, her mouth open, the phone clutched in her hand, when the man himself reefed open the door leading into his office and just stood there, staring at her as well.

She stared back, perhaps really seeing him for the first time, without those bitter blinkers she'd been wearing. Once again, she was forcibly struck by how different he was from any man Sarah had ever been involved with.

This time, however, Tina saw more than his macho physique. She saw the strength of character in his face, and the capacity for softness in his eyes.

He wasn't the stuff suave, cold-blooded seducers were made of.

In addition to having no capacity for softness, suave, cold-blooded seducers always paid attention to their appearance. Vanity was one of their many flaws.

Tina liked the fact that the navy single-breasted suit Dominic was wearing that morning was obviously off the peg; that his blue shirt wasn't lawn, or silk, or hand-made; that his tie was so out of date that any other man would have long donated it to charity.

She also liked it that he was passionate about his work, and caring of his mother, and careful now with his choice of secretary.

She liked more about Dominic Hunter's personality than she'd ever realised. And she liked Dominic Hunter, the sexy virile man, even more.

'I...I had to see you,' she blurted out, and brushed past him into his office.

She made it to his desk, where she leant on her handbag, quivering inside. She heard him quietly shut the door, then make a slow, thoughtful progress across the thick blue carpet. When he came into view, she noted he was still staring at her, his intense gaze betraying a degree of curiosity in her appearance.

She'd put her hair up and changed clothes since their appointment at the surgery, the escalating heat demanding something cooler than jeans and T-shirt. So she'd showered and put on a shift dress, light and flowery, with no sleeves, a deep round neck and a hem just above the knees. Although she'd left her legs bare, it wasn't really a provocative outfit, but it was feminine and fresh.

With Dominic's eyes on her in it, Tina felt *very* feminine, and totally flustered.

Hard to concentrate on abject apologies when every nerve-ending you owned was on instant sexual alert, when every female part in your body began tingling with an exquisitely sharp awareness.

He sat down in the big black chair behind the desk, still staring up at her.

Start saying something, she urged herself, *before you make a total mess of this.*

'I...I came to apologise,' she began, not wanting to keep looking at him but compelled by the way he was looking at her. As if he was mesmerised.

He leant forward at her opening words, his blue eyes glittering with a mixture of surprise and anticipation.

'I've been so wrong,' she blathered on. 'About you. I...I can see that now. After you left to go to work this morning, your mother told me about Damien Parsons, about the man he is…or *was*, I mean. I saw straight away he was just the kind of creep Sarah was always getting tangled up with. You're not Sarah's type at all. But…but the crunch really came when I realised his name began with a D.'

Dominic leant back in his chair, startled and puzzled. 'A D?'

'Yes.' Hurriedly she opened the bag she'd been leaning on and pulled out a pile of florist's cards. 'I found these amongst Sarah's bits and pieces. They all say the same sort of thing. Love notes. They were all signed 'D'.'

'Which you thought stood for Dominic,' he said, glancing at a couple of them. 'So you believed I sent these, along with flowers?'

'Yes…' Her voice was small. Shaky.

He looked up and their eyes met. Tears filled her.

'I'm so sorry, Dominic,' she cried. 'I jumped to conclusions which I shouldn't have. And I refused to listen to a word you said. You were right when you said Sarah must have lied about you. And you were right when you called me prejudiced. I was. I accept now that you're not Bonnie's father. Damien Parsons is. But the damage has been done, hasn't it? I've hurt you, and now I've hurt your mother. Your dear, *dear* mother.'

More tears flooded her eyes, and she was having the devil of a time blinking them away. But she was determined not to burst into hysterical weeping. What good would that do?

'I can't tell you how dreadful I feel, Dominic. I hate myself more than you do, believe me, but I…I don't know what to do for the best. I don't want to hurt any more people, least of all that man's widow and family. Do...do you happen to know if this Damien's parents are still alive?'

'No, they're not,' he said.

Tina sighed. 'I'm relieved. It would have been difficult not to give Bonnie the chance to know them, but I didn't want to upset them. I was also afraid they wouldn't want to know *her*. And I wouldn't have liked that.'

Dominic smiled a wry smile. 'No. I can imagine.'

'What about his widow? I suppose she wouldn't want to know Bonnie, either.'

'I doubt it,' he said drily. 'Look, Tina, I can't have you go on any further under these misconceptions of yours.'

She blinked her bewilderment. 'Misconceptions? What misconceptions?'

'Firstly, I do not hate you. Far from it.'

'Oh,' she said, and quivered helplessly.

'Secondly, and perhaps more important, is your misconception that Damien Parsons is Bonnie's father.'

'But...but...you said. I mean...'

'He and Sarah had an affair all right. That part's correct. Sarah probably thought he *was* the father. I'm convinced she went to him and told him of her pregnancy. I know for a fact she never mentioned my name personally to that neighbour of hers. I went back to that house in Lewisham yesterday and checked with that old lady. Betty. Sarah only said she'd been to see the father of her baby, her ex-boss. She didn't name names.'

Tina was none the wiser so far. Dominic seemed

to have proved even more conclusively that Damien *was* the father. 'So?' she probed, still puzzled.

'I believe when Damien denied being responsible and gave Sarah that money for a termination, he might not have explained the real reason why he couldn't be Bonnie's father. Maybe he simply let Sarah think he thought she was a slut and slept around. Maybe he wanted to keep the truth a secret.'

'The truth?'

'Damien had a vasectomy some years earlier because he didn't want children. He couldn't father any child, Tina, not even his own.'

Tina could not have been more shocked. 'When...when did you find this out?'

'Only this morning.'

'Who from?'

'I...can't tell you that. This is all very confidential information, Tina.'

'His poor wife. Did she know, do you think?'

'Don't waste any sympathy on Joanna Parsons,' he said sharply. 'She slept around as much as Damien. They had one of those...modern...marriages.'

Tina could not help grimacing with distaste.

'Quite,' Dominic drawled.

Tina noted his disgusted tone. Dominic really was extremely old-fashioned in some ways. One partner after another was fine by him when single, but marriage meant loyalty and commitment to one person only. Perhaps he'd always shied away from getting married because he didn't feel up to loving only the one woman for the rest of his life.

Which at least was honest.

Better he stay single than end up in a divorce court. Divorce was so hard on children, and...

'Oh!' she cried, her eyes flying to his. 'I just realised. If Damien's not Bonnie's father, then that just leaves...'

'Yes,' he finished for her, an odd smile curving his mouth. 'That just leaves yours truly.'

'But...but...why are you smiling like that? Aren't you upset? I know you don't want Bonnie.'

'Who says so?'

He actually sounded indignant!

'Why...you did!' Tina told him.

'That was just anger and shock talking,' he pronounced, waving his hand dismissively. 'I resented being accused of something I hadn't done, namely seducing Sarah then abandoning her, pregnant and practically destitute. I would never do something like that, Tina. Never!' he repeated forcibly.

'I know that now,' she said in chastened tones whilst inside her heart was singing. Dominic was Bonnie's father. Everything was going to be all right. Ida would not be devastated. Bonnie would have a good father. And she...well, she would survive, as long as she could see him sometimes. Who knew? Maybe she'd stop panting after him one day. Maybe they would end up good friends.

He stood up and began to pace up and down in front of the large window behind the desk, his hands linked behind his back, his expression serious. 'I'm not a man afraid to face up to his responsibilities,' he pronounced while he paced. 'Now that I've got used to the idea of having a child, I find I rather like it. Bonnie's a beautiful baby. And smart too. Anyone can see that. I have two good women eager to help me bring my daughter up,' he said, stopping to flash her a grateful smile. 'What more could a man want?'

'This...this is just too good to be true!' Tina exclaimed, and Dominic actually looked a little embarrassed for a moment. But only for a moment.

His eyes took on a different look altogether as he walked towards her. They narrowed and glinted with an intensity which sent another quiver all through her.

'And then, of course,' he said softly as he curved his large strong hands over her slight, slender shoulders, 'there is the added bonus of my daughter's guardian sending me into a sexual spin the like of which I have never known.' His fingers tightened and he drew her against him. 'She's doing it to me now,' he rasped. 'Looking at me with those big, dark, sexy eyes of hers, telling me of what she wants me to do, forcing me to obey their silent commands...' And his mouth began to descend.

Tina's lips parted, about to protest her innocence of such desires. But no protest came, unless one counted the small moan which escaped when their mouths met.

It was a kiss of the most passionate persuasion, his hands capturing her face and allowing her no room for anything but to return his passion, to drown in it, then go with it, riding the rapids of desire, racing on and on down the raging river of desire till its unstoppable force spilled into the ocean, its power finally spent and becalmed.

And so it was with Dominic and Tina that day.

Less than five minutes later, Tina came through the storm to find herself sitting on the edge of Dominic's desk, her legs still entwined round his hips, her mouth slowly disengaging from his, her breathing raw and ragged.

Dazed, she let her arms slip away from where

they'd been snaked around his neck, falling limply onto the shiny black surface on either side of her. She might have collapsed backwards if she hadn't grabbed at the edge of the desk. At the same time her leaden legs slipped downwards. When he withdrew, she let out a shuddering sigh, which sounded more like a groan.

His eyes searched hers while he attended to his clothes. Tina winced slightly at the sound of the zipper.

'You all right?' he asked with some concern in his voice.

'I…I don't know,' she returned shakily.

But she knew what he meant. Dominic had been less than gentle when he'd hoisted her up onto the desk, ripping off her pants before plunging into her, swift and savage in his passion.

Not that she blamed him for losing it. She'd been the one to free him from his trousers whilst he'd kissed her. She'd been the one to be utterly shameless, touching him like that.

Tina could only shake her head at herself in utter amazement, her eyes dropping in part embarrassment, part confusion. Was this the same girl who'd thought sex was boring and overrated, who'd previously felt nothing but disgust for females who were easy and fast?

No one could have been easier and faster than she had just been!

Tina would have liked to call what they'd just done lovemaking, but somehow she didn't think love ever came into the equation where Dominic and sex were concerned.

Still…she couldn't deny it had been incredibly exciting. Her eyelashes fluttered as she looked up at him, an ambivalent heat claiming her cheeks. Was she feeling shame, or more excitement?

Surely she couldn't possibly want more.

'Come on,' Dominic murmured, and gently lifted her down off the desk. 'The washroom's over there,' he directed, nodding towards a side door as he took a large lock of errant hair and tucked it behind her ear. 'I'll call you a taxi while you...um...repair any damage. Time you went home. You look like you could do with a sleep. We'll get back to this later tonight, when good little babies are fast asleep.'

Tina sucked in a startled gasp and he smiled the slowest, sexiest smile. 'You didn't think I was going to let it go at that, did you, Tina? We've had two quickies so far, both of which were fantastic but which really only whet the appetite for more. I want an opportunity to make love properly for once, at our leisure. You want that too, don't you?'

She swallowed convulsively. Dear heaven, what did he *mean* by properly? Surely he didn't mean all those shockingly intimate activities she'd read about, the ones which she couldn't believe *any* woman really enjoyed.

Yes, of course he did, came back the cool voice of reason. He was a man of the world. And after the way she'd acted last night—and today—he believed her to be a *woman* of the world.

The thought had her nervously licking her lips.

'I can see you do,' he misinterpreted, and bent to brush his lips over her trembling ones. 'It's going to be so hard trying to work for the rest of the day,' he murmured. 'Thinking of tonight... Thinking of you... Thinking of this...'

And he kissed her again.

CHAPTER FIFTEEN

THE taxi delivered Tina to the door, Ida coming down to the front gate to meet her, Bonnie hoisted happily over her shoulder.

'So how did it go?' she asked, her intuitive blue eyes giving a still stunned Tina a curious once-over. 'You don't look all that happy. Did you sort out whatever it was you had to sort out with Dominic?'

The question put Tina's distracted mind back on track. Any personal problems she had with Dominic were irrelevant in the face of the big picture, which was that Bonnie's future, and Ida's happiness, were assured.

'Yes, I did,' she said, smiling at Ida as she took Bonnie into her arms. 'Once we really talked, your son agreed it was very likely he was Bonnie's father, and that Damien Parsons wasn't. The timing was all wrong for it to be Damien's,' Tina invented, since she didn't have permission to mention the vasectomy.

'Timing, schiming,' Ida tossed back impatiently. 'You only have to look at little Bonnie there to see she's Dominic's. She has the Hunter genes stamped all over her.'

Privately, Tina still thought Bonnie was *nothing* like Dominic. She was dainty and fair and ultra-feminine, just like Sarah. But who was she to spoil a grandmother's pleasure in her granddaughter?

'If he'd listened to reason, I could have pointed out all the evidence for his own blind eyes,' Ida swept

on, 'but he was being so pig-headed that I thought it
would do him good to stew in his own juice till the
tests came back, and then he'd have egg all over his
face. I'm almost sorry he's now facing up his respon-
sibility. I was rather looking forward to him looking
a little foolish for once.'

'I can't imagine Dominic ever looking foolish,'
Tina murmured as they walked towards the house.

'He certainly did last Friday,' Ida said drily. 'You
rattled his sabre, I can tell you.'

Tina thought that was a very apt turn of phrase.
She certainly *had*. But he'd soon found a scabbard
for that rattling sabre, hadn't he? Hers truly.

'Dominic has this ingrained determination to control everything in his life,' Ida raved on. 'No doubt
this change of heart is him still trying to do that. Today at the surgery made him face that soon he
wouldn't be able to pretend he *wasn't* Bonnie's father. That the test would prove differently. I'll bet he
decided to embrace the truth first, so that he feels in
control again. Dominic has to be the boss of everything, you know. When he's being his most nice and
reasonable, he's at his most dangerous and devious.
Was he nice and reasonable to you when you got in
there to see him?'

'Well...um...yes, I suppose he was. In a way...'

'Then watch yourself. He's probably planning how
to get you to do exactly what he wants.'

Tina's mouth went dry at the thought of what
Dominic wanted tonight.

Ida opened the front door for her without drawing
breath. 'No doubt he's trying to organise his life so
that Bonnie will make the least amount of change to
his routine. He's sure to ask you to move in here

permanently now, so that he has two women on tap to do all the baby-minding. Dominic will be a responsible father, but not in a full-time hands-on way. That would interfere with his work!'

Tina dragged her mind back from the abyss to listen to what Ida was saying.

'*Nothing* is allowed to interfere with my son's work, not even his extra-curricular activities. Why do you think I didn't know about that Shani woman? Because he slots sex into his life like his dental appointments—well after office hours or during his lunchbreak. Yes, you can look shocked, but I've seen his bank card statement. How else can you explain bills for city hotel rooms when I know full well he came home those nights and was working in his office all those days, except lunchtime?'

They were by then standing in the blessedly cool hallway, at the bottom of the stairs. Tina's eyes were wide on Ida, and her heart was racing. If what Dominic's mother was saying was true, then *she* was about to be slotted into Dominic's life even more conveniently than Shani. He wouldn't even have to leave the house to have sex with *her*!

'*Has* he asked you to move in here?' Ida asked.

'No.'

Ida nodded wryly. 'He will, dear. He will. And when he does, what will your answer be?'

Tina could tell that, despite Ida's critical attitude towards her son, she was eager for her to say yes. And, really, it was the perfect solution all round. If she and Dominic hadn't become lovers, she would not have had second thoughts.

But they *had* become lovers, and nothing would change that.

Tina was beginning to appreciate how weak a woman could become when in the grip of a sexual infatuation.

She refused to call it love. Sarah had always called her infatuations 'love', but time had always proved her wrong.

Still, Tina could certainly understand why a girl like Sarah had been out of her depth if she'd felt like this all the time. It was difficult to stay strong, and independent-minded; difficult to ignore the yearnings Dominic had set up within her body.

'What will I say?' she said, and sighed in recognition of her own weak flesh. 'I'll say yes, I suppose.'

Ida beamed. 'That's what I'd hoped you say. Here now, give me Bonnie back and you go upstairs and have a nap. You look awfully tired, dear.'

'I am, Ida. I am.'

Dominic felt some alarm when he came home that night. Tina was acting strangely with him, tensing up whenever he came within three feet of her. She seemed to deliberately avoid being alone with him, using the baby or his mother to keep him from having the opportunity to speak to her privately, or to even steal a simple kiss.

And he wanted to kiss her. He wanted to kiss her very badly.

The three of them sat down to dinner at seven-thirty, with the pram pulled up beside him, Bonnie inside.

Dominic had insisted, hoping to impress Tina with this sudden burst of fatherly attention. She hadn't seemed impressed, however. She remained distracted and tense all through the meal. Even his coochiecooing the baby occasionally hadn't raised much more than a tight little smile.

'Did you manage to get some sleep this afternoon?' he asked when his mother left the table to get the coffee pot.

Immediately her shoulders stiffened and her eyes skittered away from his. 'A little...'

'Tina, what *is* it?' he asked, but she didn't answer. 'Is it something I've done, or not done?'

She shook her head.

'Is this your way of telling me you don't want to come to my room later?'

Her head whipped back, her eyes shocked yet glittering. '*Your* room?' she said huskily.

Any fear he'd had that she no longer wanted him was firmly routed. He understood where she was coming from now. Underneath, she was as excited as he was. But she wasn't as sure of herself sexually as their raw encounter in the office earlier in the day might have suggested.

Dominic suspected that Tina was essentially a shy girl, with few lovers in the past and a deep distrust of the opposite sex. He would have to be careful tonight, and not frighten her with demands beyond her limited experience.

Not that he was looking for just sex. He wanted so much more than that.

'It's further away from the stairs,' he explained softly. 'And it has a lock on the door.'

'But I won't be able to hear Bonnie from there if she cries.'

Incredible, he thought. She was practically quivering with desire, but she still thought of the baby. What power this little child had!

Of course, Bonnie *was* a sweet little thing. Very pretty and very engaging. Anyone could easily become entranced by her winning little smiles.

'I've asked Mum to keep Bonnie downstairs with her tonight,' he told a startled Tina. 'She said she was going to suggest it herself. She said you needed a good night's sleep, and naturally I agreed.'

Tina trembled at the wickedness of the man. He had it all thought out, didn't he? All planned, as Ida had said. Nothing was to be allowed to interrupt his pleasure.

Or hers, came the added corrupting thought.

Devious and dangerous, his mother had called him. She was right there. He wanted what he wanted, when he wanted it.

The trouble was, she was a willing victim of what he wanted at the moment. But what would happen when he tired of her? When the sex grew boring and some new and more exciting woman walked into his life?

She'd swiftly supplanted Shani, after all.

One day someone would supplant her.

Who next? she wondered. Joanna Parsons, perhaps? Or had he already tasted that particular pie?

No, no, he would not seduce another man's wife. That was not Dominic's way. He had his own moral code when it came to sex and it didn't include adultery.

'What on earth are you thinking about?' he asked a tad irritably, just as his mother came back into the room, carrying the coffee pot.

Tina decided to take back some control over her life, at least superficially. 'I was thinking it might be a good idea if I moved in here on a semi-permanent basis,' she said, before Dominic had a chance to ask. Or coerce. 'What do you think, Ida? After all, it's *your* house.'

Ida threw her an admiring glance. 'I think that's a splendid idea. That way we can share the babysitting. All three of us.'

Tina watched Dominic as his mother's words sank in. 'All *three* of us?' he repeated, frowning.

'Yes, of course,' Ida returned sweetly as she poured the coffee. 'You're Bonnie's father, after all. You have to do your share.'

'Mmm. I don't have much time for babysitting, you know. I work very long hours.'

Ida exchanged knowing looks with Tina. 'Really? Well, maybe you'll have to work less long hours in future.'

His smile was as sudden as it was unexpected. 'You're absolutely right. I will. But not tonight, I'm afraid. Tonight I've brought some important work home with me which needs my urgent attention. To-morrow night, however, I'm all yours. Night-night, sweetie.' He blew Bonnie a kiss before scraping his chair back and rising to his feet. 'I'll be in my room if I'm desperately needed.'

Tina's stomach contracted at his choice of words, and she steadfastly avoided his eyes as he left the room, his coffee in hand.

She busied herself spooning some sugar into her own coffee, then adding cream. 'Seems you were wrong, Ida,' she said casually whilst her insides were in knots. 'He's going to do his bit.'

'You think so? Remember what I said, Tina. When Dominic is being nice and co-operative, he's up to something. Some secret agenda of his own. Don't ever...*ever* underestimate him.'

Tina didn't. But she thought Ida was being a little harsh. Dominic had been very good since finding out he was Bonnie's father.

Well, not good exactly. A *good* man wouldn't have had her on his desk in twenty seconds flat today. A *good* man would not manipulate his mother to mind his baby so that he could have his wicked way with his baby's guardian half the night long.

Tina's spoon rattled in the cup as she stirred in the sugar. How long could she delay, she wondered agitatedly, before Dominic came to her room tonight and dragged her down to his?

CHAPTER SIXTEEN

THE bedside clock said eleven-thirteen. Tina had stayed downstairs watching television with Ida till ten-thirty, at which point Ida had announced she'd best get to bed. Bonnie had had a bottle at nine-thirty and would wake again around two or three. When Tina had promised to be downstairs for the morning feed, Ida had told her not to be so silly.

'I'm not so old that I can't remember how it feels to be sleep-deprived. You sleep in as late as you like for once. If I get desperate by morning, I'll go get Bonnie's father up bright and early to help. I'm sure he'll be thrilled,' she'd cackled.

Tina hadn't dared say anything to this. But she vowed not to be tricked into spending the whole night in Dominic's bed.

If she ever *reached* his bed. At that moment she was sitting on the side of her own bed, body showered and legs smooth, skin powdered and erogenous zones perfumed.

She'd felt hopelessly turned on during all these erotic preparations, her hands shaking so much while she'd shaved her legs that she was lucky not to have nicks all over her.

Now, she just felt sick.

Time ticked by towards midnight, which seemed to her the deadline for staying in her room. Dominic would surely come to see where she was after midnight. And, when he did, the humiliation would be greater than any endured by going to his room first.

Swallowing, Tina rose and walked towards the door.

Dominic tried not to clock-watch. After his second cold shower of the night, he sat at his computer, pretending to work, when all the while he was listening for Tina. It was nearly midnight, damn it! Surely she was going to come. Surely.

And then he heard something: the soft squeaks of a door being opened and closed. He strained his ears and thought he heard the soft fall of her footsteps coming down the hall, at which point he could not stay sitting a moment longer. Leaping up, he swept open his door and found himself looking down into her upturned eyes, her wide, dark, fear-filled eyes.

With a groan, he reached out to cup her frightened face, drawing her towards him and upwards till she was on tiptoe and their mouths were almost touching.

'There's nothing to be afraid of,' he whispered. 'Nothing at all...'

Tina had to give him credit. He knew all the right moves and said all the right things.

At his soft touch and equally soft words her fears were scattered, and all she wanted was to sink against his hard male body and surrender to its power.

Which was exactly what she did. And oh...how wonderful he felt. And how wonderful he smelt, his skin freshly washed, with just a splash of expensive cologne.

His first kiss was hungry and long, their mouths staying glued while he angled her inside and locked the door behind them. His second kiss was softer, yet just as seductive, his hands expertly divesting her of her wrap and nightie without missing a beat.

Once she was naked, a long tremor ran down Tina's spine, and Dominic drew back to look at her.

'Don't tell me you don't like showing off this perfect body of yours,' he murmured.

Tina had never thought her body perfect. It was a far cry from the hourglass shape and voluptuous breasts men seemed to favour, and which Sarah had been blessed with. Though perhaps Sarah's figure had been more of a curse than a blessing.

'You like my body?' came her surprised reply.

'I adore it,' he growled, and scooped her up into his large strong arms. 'I love your small breasts and your slender hips. I love your flat stomach and your tight little butt. I especially love your long legs and your slender ankles. Hell, I love everything about you, woman. I thought you knew that.'

He carried her quickly to the bed, where he lowered her onto the crisp clean sheets and snowy pillows. He tossed aside his black silk robe as if it was a rag and would have joined her on the bed still wearing his pyjama bottoms, if Tina hadn't protested.

'No, no,' she said with a boldness which shocked and excited her at the same time. 'I want you naked too.'

His eyebrows arched, but he didn't seem to mind complying.

And why would he? she thought breathlessly as her eyes roved hotly over him, this time without skittering nervously away. The man was magnificent.

'Do...do you work out a lot?' she asked, once he'd lain down beside her. Tina had automatically rolled onto her side, and Dominic did likewise, propping himself up on one elbow.

'Some,' he said. 'It relieves stress. There's a convenient gym in my building.'

'And the all-over tan?'

'Sunbed.'

He smiled and she frowned. 'What's so funny?'

'I don't usually like to talk when I'm in bed with a woman.'

'Oh.' Suddenly she felt foolish. And shy. If she could have fled, she would have.

'But I like talking to you, my darling Tina,' he went on, reaching out to stroke a soft hand down her arm and over her hip onto her thigh. She could not believe what a turn-on she found such a simple gesture.

'I like it so much,' he murmured, 'that I could just talk to you and touch you all night.' His hand kept moving, trailing up and down her body. 'Would you like that, my love?' he crooned in a voice almost as mesmerising as his hand, which at that moment was trickling over her breasts, teasing their expectant nipples. 'You wouldn't have to do a thing. Just lie back, close your eyes and enjoy...'

And somehow, in no time, that was exactly what she was doing, lying on her back and enjoying, with his hand finding increasingly intimate places and his voice in her ear promising her the most incredible pleasures if only she'd trust him. With his erotic whispers and caresses, she felt every vestige of control slip away, every fear, every inhibition. When his hand stopped and his mouth took over, protesting never entered Tina's mind.

And so it was for the next few hours.

Dominic made love to her several times, surprising Tina with his gentleness, but also with his stamina. He could not seem to get enough of her body. Touching it. Tasting it. Taking it. Over and over. Her fears about what he might demand of her never eventuated. He didn't make any demands she couldn't meet. In fact, he didn't make any demands on her at all except to surrender to what he wanted to do to *her* body, which, though stunningly intimate, never crossed the line into anything which made her uncomfortable.

Between times, they talked, telling each other the silliest little things, sharing childhood experiences, exchanging compliments. Lovers' talk, Tina supposed. But it was nice. So very nice. She could almost imagine Dominic genuinely cared about her, that he wanted to spend time with her even when they weren't making love.

When he finally fell asleep, Tina lay there for quite some time, trying to come to terms with all that had just happened.

Was it still just sex? she pondered.

Not for her, came back the honest answer.

But it probably was for him. Why else would he be going about it like this, in the dead of night? No, he wasn't in love with her. She was just his latest sex partner, being slotted into his life with the least amount of time or trouble.

Sighing, she slipped from between the sheets, dressed, then snuck quietly back to her room where, surprisingly, she fell asleep as soon as her head hit the pillow. When she finally made it downstairs around noon, Tina was amazed to learn that Dominic had been up at seven as usual.

'He was in such a good mood,' Ida informed her

over brunch. 'He even took time to give Bonnie her bottle, then asked me to show him how to change her nappy. Did it like a champion on his first go and was ever so pleased with himself. If I didn't know better, I'd think he might actually get to *like* being a father.'

Tina could only shake her head. Dominic was an enigma all right. She didn't know what to make of him.

'And another thing,' Ida went on. 'You know the doctor said we had to bring Bonnie back this week for her three-month vaccinations.'

'Yes.'

'Well, I made an appointment for first thing Thursday morning, and guess what?'

'What?'

'Dominic wants to take you and Bonnie himself.'

Tina frowned. 'But he'll be late for work.'

'That's what I said. But he said that didn't matter. He said you might need him. He said he saw how upset you got when they took Bonnie's blood yesterday.'

Tina had to admit she did feel anxious about taking Bonnie for another needle. She would rather have fifty injections herself than watch her little charge have one. Still, she was surprised by Dominic's having been this observant of her feelings.

'That's very…thoughtful…of him,' she said, wondering if she had misjudged the man.

'Yes, it is,' Ida said, then pursed her lips. 'I wish I could work out what he's up to.'

'Maybe he's not up to anything,' Tina defended. 'Maybe he really cares about Bonnie now that he knows she is.'

'Yes. Yes, that's possible, I suppose. I always believed he had the makings of a good father in him somewhere.'

Tina hoped she was right.

Dominic felt Bonnie's shock and pain the moment the needle started to go into her thigh.

And why not? The darned thing was *huge*! He wouldn't have liked to have it himself. His heart twisted when she flinched in his arms, then started to cry.

Dear God, he felt like a monster, an inhuman, cruel monster, holding her there to be tortured. It was an illogical reaction, he knew. Vaccinations were essential for any child's well-being. Without them, she might succumb to any of a number of childhood diseases.

But logic didn't seem to play a part in how he was feeling as he tried to hold a struggling Bonnie still. Afterwards, he walked her around the room and did his best to soothe her loud sobbing.

'There, there, darling. Don't cry. Daddy's here.'

Dominic pulled himself up with a jolt.

Daddy?

My God, had he really said that?

Daddy, he mused as he rubbed Bonnie's back.

The word stirred something in him. Made him feel all soft, yet strong at the same time.

'Sorry about that,' the doctor excused once Bonnie's sobs had subsided to hiccups. 'But it's all for the best.'

'Easy to say when you're on the other end of the needle,' Dominic grumped.

'I guess so.' The doctor gave Dominic a sharp look.

'Am I to presume you're no longer questioning the child's parentage?'

Dominic was about to tell him he could cancel the test when Tina burst into the room, her eyes agitated and shimmering. 'I couldn't stand listening to her cry like that. Is she all right?'

'She's fine,' the doctor said. 'Her daddy here has things firmly in hand.'

Dominic wasn't too sure of that. He'd just missed his chance to tell the doctor to cancel the test, and now he had a teary Tina looking at him with distress and scepticism in her eyes. Admittedly, Bonnie *had* begun to cry again.

'Give her to me,' Tina demanded, and swept the child from his arms.

Dominic watched, somewhat disgruntled, when the baby quietened immediately. It seemed he still had some way to go before he won the award for Father of the Year.

'Bonnie might run a little temperature during the next twenty-four hours,' the doctor warned. 'If she does, then give her some infant's paracetamol. Other than that, everything should be fine.'

'Fine, my foot,' Dominic muttered as he trailed after Tina, who was already hurrying through the waiting room full of coughing, wheezing people.

He'd thought she trusted him now, thought she might even be falling in love with him.

Now he wasn't so sure...

Bonnie went to sleep as soon as the car moved off, bringing about an awkward silence between its two adult occupants.

Tina didn't say a word.

Dominic could not understand her mood. She'd seemed fine the night before.

'Is there anything wrong, Tina?' he finally asked.

'No. What could possibly be wrong?'

He frowned. 'Is that sarcasm I hear?'

She sighed and turned her head away.

When he jerked the car over to the kerb and cut the engine, her head whipped round to glower at him. 'What do you think you're doing? You'll be even later for work now!'

'Work can wait.'

'Well, that's a new one, according to your mother.'

'Oh? And what *else* has my darling mother had to say behind my back?'

'Nothing I didn't already know.'

'Such as?'

'Such as your attitude to women and sex.'

'Which is what?'

'You know very well what your attitude to women and sex is, Dominic. I overheard you voice it the very first night I met you. Perhaps your past women have gone in for cold-blooded, sex-only affairs, but I find I don't like it one bit. In fact, I'm very angry with myself for letting you use me in that way.' Once again, she turned her head away from him.

'But I'm not using you,' he denied, panic-stricken at the way this conversation was going.

'Yeah, right,' she snapped.

'Look at me, Tina,' he pleaded. 'And try to listen to what I'm saying.'

She actually gave him one of those contemptuous looks which had first turned him on. Now, it churned his stomach.

'I'm listening,' she said coldly.

Dominic hesitated, not sure where to start. It was too early to tell her he loved her. She wouldn't believe him. He knew it. But he wanted her to know she was special to him, not just a convenient lay.

Hell, he'd handled this all very badly. In hindsight, he could see slipping into her bed after lights out the last two nights didn't make him look good, especially as he'd left her bed after the lovemaking was over. No wonder she thought all he wanted from her was sex.

But he'd mistakenly believed that was what *she* wanted at this point in their relationship.

He wasn't used to being with a woman who wanted more. He wasn't used to *himself* wanting for. Frankly, he just didn't know how to conduct a normal relationship with a woman.

But he had to learn. And quickly.

Unclipping his seat belt, he reached over to take her hands in his, steadfastly ignoring the instant wariness on her face. 'What I feel for you, Tina,' he said with genuine feeling, 'is so much more than just sex. I told you once before I thought what we had was special. You think so too, *don't* you? I can tell you're not the sort of woman who jumps into bed with just anyone, no matter what you said last Monday night.'

She looked oddly discomfited by his words. 'Is it that obvious?'

'Is what that obvious?'

'That I'm pretty hopeless in bed.'

'What on earth are you talking about? You're not hopeless in bed. You're a darling in bed. So warm and responsive. You make me feel like a king.'

'But I...I haven't done any of those things men

really like. I mean...oh, you know what I mean, Dominic.'

'But I haven't *wanted* you to,' he insisted in all honesty. 'It's given me such pleasure to give *you* pleasure. Oh, my darling, darling Tina,' he murmured, lifting her fingers to kiss them. 'You have no idea what just being with you does to me. I have no need of fancy positions or kinky foreplay. All I need is your lovely mouth on mine and I'm in heaven.'

Her big dark eyes searched his face with a desperation he found infinitely reassuring. 'Then why am I a secret, Dominic? Why do we have to sneak into each other's beds. Make me understand that and I'll believe you.'

'I can only apologise for that. I have to confess to some terrible habits when it comes to the women in my life so far. I've been appallingly selfish. My only excuse is that I didn't want to turn out like my father.'

'Your father?'

'Yes. He was an incorrigible philanderer, then tried to justify everything by claiming he'd *fallen in love* with all his other women. He claimed he couldn't help himself. God, I despised him, especially for what he did to Mum. How she kept loving him, and forgiving him, I'll never know.'

'You know...that's how I used to feel about Sarah. I couldn't understand why she let the men in her life treat her so badly...all in the name of *love*.'

'So you vowed not to be like her,' Dominic muttered, thinking he could well understand that. *He'd* vowed never to be like his father, whom he'd thought a fool of the first order, not only in his personal life but in business. A stockbroker too, he'd taken such stupid risks, both with his own money and his clients'. When he'd died, the family firm, as well as the family finances, had been in a damned awful mess.

But that was all in the past, Dominic realised, brushing aside any bitter thoughts. He had the here and now to worry about.

'Let's start again, shall we?' he suggested.

A startled Tina stared at him. 'In what way?'

'We'll go out, like a normal couple.'

Her eyes lit up. 'Date, you mean?'

'Yes. Starting tomorrow night. You get all dressed up and I'll take you to a fancy restaurant for dinner. That way Mum will know we're getting on well, and it won't come as a shock once she eventually realises we're more than just good friends.'

'But...but what about the bedroom arrangements? I mean...'

'We'll cross that bridge when we come to it.'

'Knowing you,' she said a little drily, 'we'll come to it later tonight.'

'Ahh no, I don't think so,' he said, smiling.

'You're too tired?' she returned, looking deliciously disappointed.

'No. It's Mum's bridge night tonight. She'll be gone from the house by seven-thirty.'

He watched the instant excitement leap into her eyes and thought perhaps it was time Tina's sexual experience was extended. He couldn't really have her thinking she was hopeless in bed. Or out of it!

CHAPTER SEVENTEEN

'I STILL don't believe it!' Ida exclaimed excitedly. 'Dominic asked you out and you actually said yes! I mean, I knew you'd mellowed a bit towards him this past week, and I *always* knew you were his type, but I never hoped...never expected...' She sank down onto the side of Tina's bed, holding a hand over her heart. 'It's too much.'

Tina turned from where she'd been titivating herself in the dressing table mirror for ages.

'Now don't get your hopes up too high, Ida,' she warned gently. 'Dominic is still Dominic.'

'But you like him, don't you? You really, really like him.'

'I really, really like him.'

'More than like, I'll warrant,' Ida said with sly glint in her eyes. 'He's a sexy beast, is my son.'

'That he is,' Tina agreed, a shiver running down her spine. 'Beast' was the exact word to describe him last night. Ida had barely left the house when he'd pounced. Thank the Lord Bonnie had been upstairs asleep at the time.

'Not in bed,' he'd growled as he'd grabbed her from behind, his mouth clamping down into her throat.

Bed had certainly not figured in their lovemaking that evening. The change of scene had brought a change in Dominic's needs. Suddenly he'd wanted more from her. Surprisingly, so had she wanted to give more.

Tina was still stunned at how willingly she'd done what she'd thought she would never do with a man. Yet doing it had seemed to liberate her to want so much more, finding the wildest excitement in Dominic's making love to her in all sorts of exotic positions and places. She'd been utterly shameless. And quite demanding in her own right.

Even now, although the memories still slightly shocked her, she felt no shame. For she loved Dominic. How could anything be wrong when you loved someone?

But did he love her in return?

He hadn't said so. Even if he had, would she have believed him? Men often said they loved a woman when they didn't. It was sex they wanted in the main, not love. Sarah's many one-sided love affairs had taught Tina that.

But she could not deny she had her hopes. Just as Ida did. Best she heed her own warnings, however, and not let those hopes get too high.

'So how do you think I look?' she asked Ida.

'Beautiful,' Ida praised. 'Just beautiful!'

Actually, Tina thought she looked pretty good too. She didn't have a lot of dressy clothes—she lived in jeans and pants most of the time—but what she had was of the best quality.

The dress she was wearing was a simple black number in an uncrushable material which looked like a cross between velvet and suede. The style was an elegant sheath of simple lines, cut in at the shoulders, with a high, round neckline. It was short without being too short. Tight without being too tight. When combined with black strappy high heels and dangling rhinestone earrings, the dress looked a million dollars.

'Dominic's going to drool when he sees you,' Ida said. 'I hope you know what you're doing.'

'What do you mean?'

'My dear, my son is not one to play the gentleman with a beautiful woman for too long, especially if she dolls herself up for him.'

'Ida,' Tina told her firmly. 'I'm twenty-six years old. I've been around. I know exactly what I'm doing.'

Ida's eyebrows arched. 'Well, well, well. Still, do be careful, love. I wouldn't like to see you get hurt. Men can be so selfish sometimes, telling a girl they love them when in fact all they really want to do is get them into bed.'

Tina sighed. Too true, Ida. Too true.

'Your mother thinks you're an incorrigible rake.'

Dominic's teeth clenched down hard in his jaw. Slowly, he put down his wine glass and surveyed the woman he loved. She looked so beautiful tonight, and so desirable. When he'd first seen her on coming home he'd been quite overcome by the trouble she'd taken with her appearance. Surely this was what a woman did for the man she loved.

This belief came from the fact he himself had raced out at lunchtime and bought some new clothes. Knowing his limitations in matters of fashion, he'd asked the elegantly dressed salesman to direct him to what would suit him and be stylish at the same time. He'd never been interested in how he looked before. But he wanted to look good for Tina. Hell, he wanted to take her breath away.

And he had. But along with her admiration for his new look had come a return to wariness, betraying a lack of trust in him. So different from the way she'd acted the previous night. She'd been so incredible, so passionate and uninhibited and, yes, trusting. He'd hoped her responses and behaviour meant he'd won more than her desire. He'd hoped love would surely follow.

Now it seemed he was back to square one. And all because of his mother, the one woman who should have been fostering their relationship, not sabotaging it. He would have to have a few words with her when he got home tonight, before any more damage was done.

'She probably thinks that because of Dad,' he said carefully. 'But she's wrong. I'm no rake. Just a fool who's finally woken up to himself.'

'Meaning?'

He looked at her hard and decided to take his destiny into his hands, with courage and no more games. 'I was going to wait a bit longer before telling you this, Tina, but the truth is I've fallen in love with you. Hard.'

She looked as if she might faint. Her hand trembled so much that some wine spilt from her glass, splashing over the white linen tablecloth.

'You...you don't mean that,' she said, her face pale, her voice shaking.

'I do. I've known it since last Monday, when you came into my office, but I thought it was too premature to say anything back then. If I've made a mistake making love to you as much as I've been doing, then I sincerely apologise. I was trying to get you to fall in love with me in return. Clearly, by the look on your face, I've failed.'

'Oh, no,' she cried, and his heart leapt into his mouth. 'You haven't failed. I...I *do* love you. I've known since last Monday as well. I just didn't dare believe...or hope...that you loved me back. But are you sure, Dominic? I mean...'

Dominic reached out to take her hand across the table, crushing it in both of his. 'I'm *very* sure. I'd do anything for you. And I mean anything,' he muttered, thinking of the lies he'd told and the way he'd pretended with the baby.

No not entirely pretended, he amended swiftly. He *did* feel something for the child.

A tap on his shoulder had him withdrawing his hands from Tina's and lifting irritable eyes. A waiter was hovering with a mobile phone in his hands.

'Sorry to interrupt your meal, Mr Hunter,' the young man said apologetically. 'But there's a phone-call for you. An emergency, the lady says.'

An emergency? Dominic took the phone, thinking that the only person who knew where he was tonight was his mother.

'Dominic Hunter,' he said somewhat testily down the line.

'Oh, Dominic, I'm so glad I reached you. I was terrified you might have gone on somewhere else.'

Dominic's stomach tightened at the near panic in his mother's voice. 'What is it, Mum?' he asked, and immediately heard Tina's sharp intake of breath.

Their eyes met across the table while he listened to his mother's distressed explanation with escalating alarm.

Apparently Bonnie had woken around nine with

what looked like the beginnings of a cold. She'd been coughing and her temperature had been up slightly. Ida given her some paracetamol. But by ten she'd started having difficulty breathing. Worried that it might be an allergic reaction to the vaccination, Ida had called the doctor, who'd said it didn't sound like that and suggested she take the baby straight to Casualty at the nearest large hospital. Apparently they'd taken one look at Bonnie and whisked her straight into Intensive Care.

'What hospital?' Dominic asked, a jolt of fear-filled adrenaline putting urgency in his voice. Dear God, if anything happened to Bonnie, Tina would just die!

'Royal North Shore.'

'We'll be there as quickly as we can,' he said, simultaneously rising to his feet.

Tina was already up, her purse in hand. Dominic took her elbow and began steering her between the busy tables.

'Have to go,' he told the waiter on the way by. 'Family emergency. Get the boss to send me a bill. He knows I'm good for it.'

'It's Bonnie, isn't it?' Tina choked out as they hurried outside the restaurant into the balmy night air. 'She's sick.'

'Yes.'

'What is it?'

'I don't know. She's coughing and having trouble breathing. Maybe it's asthma, or something like that.'

'Oh, dear God…'

Dominic took a moment to turn Tina his way, placing solid and hopefully calming hands on her shoulders. 'Now don't panic, Tina. Mum's taken her to a very good hospital. She'll be all right.'

'How can you *say* that? She might not be. She might die!'

'She can't die,' he muttered and, gripping Tina's elbow, ushered her towards the car.

It was a nightmare drive to the hospital, with a silent and ashen-faced Tina beside him and his thoughts all a-jumble. Because his worries weren't just for the woman he loved but the child herself. She was so little and so precious, to *all* of them. Surely God wouldn't take her. Surely not...

As they drew closer to the hospital Dominic began to really pray for the first time in his life. He was even driven to try to bargain with the Almighty.

Spare this innocent child, God, and I'll...I'll...

What? he thought with self-disgust. Be a good boy in future? Go to church every Sunday? Tell Tina the truth...that Damien Parsons hadn't had a vasectomy? That he'd lied about that, then used his assured position as Bonnie's father to look good in her eyes?

What would be the point in such a confession?

Tina would stop loving him, and he couldn't bear that.

But a relationship shouldn't be built on lies and deceit, came back the alternative argument.

Oh, hell, he thought!

His mother was waiting for them at the main door, looking older than he'd ever seen her look. Her eyes were haunted as she looked at Tina.

'I feel so guilty,' she blurted out. 'I think she might have been awake for some time before I heard her. I was talking on the telephone for quite a while, and it's some way from where Bonnie was sleeping.'

'Don't go blaming yourself for anything, Ida,' Tina said gently. 'We don't.'

'Where is she?' Dominic demanded.

'I'll take you to her,' she said, and off they went, a wretched little threesome if ever there was one.

Ida led them down various corridors, which echoed to their anxious steps, and finally into a room where little Bonnie lay in what looked like an oxygen tent, such a tiny thing amongst a lot of medical paraphernalia.

Tina promptly burst into tears and Dominic put his arms around her, his heart almost breaking as he gathered her close.

The nurse, who'd been standing beside the bed, ushered them out of the room. 'Are you the parents?' she asked.

'This is Bonnie's guardian,' Dominic volunteered whilst Tina sobbed against his chest. 'Her mother's dead. But I'm the father,' he added, thinking this wasn't the time for any confessions. The Lord would just have to do his best for Bonnie without any bribes.

'And I'm the grandmother,' Ida piped up. 'I brought her in.'

'And thank goodness you did,' the nurse said. 'She's a pretty sick little girl. Some new strain of bronchiolitis. Strikes very quickly. She's not doing too badly now that she can breathe more easily, but it's going to be long night. The doctor should be back shortly to check on her again. Meanwhile, try not to worry. It's good that she's not allergic to penicillin. Not that it'll kill the virus, but it's the best antibiotic for any secondary infections. Pneumonia can be a problem in these cases, we find, especially with a tot as young as this.'

'How did you know she wasn't allergic to penicillin?' Dominic asked.

The nurse looked momentarily confused. 'It's on her chart. Someone must have supplied that information when she was brought in.'

They all looked at Ida, who immediately became defensive. 'I didn't say she wasn't for sure. I just said her father wasn't allergic to it, and that it didn't run in the family.'

'For pity's sake, Mum!' Dominic exploded. 'What if I'm *not* Bonnie's father? We're not one hundred per cent sure yet, you know.'

Tina lifted her tearstained face to his. 'But, Dominic, you *must* be. Who else is there?'

'Not to worry,' the nurse hastily intervened. 'She hasn't been any antibiotics yet. We're waiting on some blood tests. Look, I'll strike that information from the chart, but I suggest you tell the doctor when you see him what the situation is regarding her known medical history. Now, I'm sorry, but I must get back to my patient.'

She bustled back into the room, leaving Dominic with the two women staring up at him. 'I just meant we couldn't be absolutely sure,' he muttered. 'Not till the test results come back.'

'But you *can*, Dominic,' Ida insisted. 'I have a piece of news for you which puts Bonnie's parenthood beyond any doubt whatsoever. That phone call I felt guilty about tonight. It was to Joanna. I wanted to explain about Bonnie, and why I hadn't invited her to dinner again after cancelling last Friday night. Anyway, she started telling me how she would have liked to have had a baby, but that Damien despised children and had had one of those operations to make sure he didn't. A vis...ves...vis...'

'A vasectomy,' Dominic said, hoping he didn't sound as stunned as he felt.

'Yes, that's it. So you see, Dominic? Damien couldn't possibly be Bonnie's father.'

Dominic must have looked strange, because Tina asked if he was all right.

He blinked, then just stared down at her, his mind a mess.

'It's just hit you for real, hasn't it?' she said softly, her lovely eyes lustrous with tears. 'That it's really *your* baby daughter lying in there.'

Oh, God, he thought. If only she knew!

'Yes,' he managed, and his mind turned to the tiny scrap of humanity lying in that room.

He'd thought he cared about her before, but the knowledge that she *was* his child evoked feelings he'd never have imagined. His level of anguish and worry went up a thousandfold. An ache claimed his heart and squeezed and squeezed, till he wanted to cry out with the pain.

Dear God, he would do *anything* to make her well, to have her come home with them, safe and sound. He would even tell Tina the truth, if it would make any difference to the powers that be.

And who knew? Maybe it would!

'I...I need to talk to you, Tina,' he said, his voice strained, his throat thick. 'Mum, do you think you could give me a few minutes alone with Tina?'

'I'll go sit with Bonnie,' she offered.

'What is it, Dominic?' Tina asked as soon as they were alone.

'I have something to tell you. Something important.'

'What?'

'I lied to you.'

Her hand fluttered up to her throat. 'Lied? You…you mean…you…you *don't* love me?'

'No, no. Of course I love you. I love you so much that that's why I lied. About the vasectomy.'

'But Dominic… That doesn't make sense. I'm very confused.'

'When I told you Damien had had a vasectomy it was because I believed he *was* the father. I'd just realised how much I loved you and I ruthlessly decided to use every means at my disposal to win your love. I invented that story about the vasectomy and claimed Bonnie was my own because I thought being Bonnie's father would help win you. You could have knocked me over with a feather when Mum said what she said just now.'

'So you really just found out she's yours?'

'Yes.'

'So all that good father stuff was just an act?'

'Yes. No. Well…in a way.' He sighed. 'Oh, I could water my guilt down and say I truly did grow fond of the child. Which is true. I did. But it was still wrong of me.'

'Dangerous and devious,' she mumbled, shaking her head and looking down at the floor.

But then her head snapped up, and she was frowning at him as though trying to work out something. 'Why are you telling me this now? You didn't *have* to.'

He shrugged, feeling both helpless and hopeless. 'I had this crazy idea that maybe God is punishing me, that maybe I could make Bonnie well if I told you the truth. Then there's another voice in my head which keeps telling me a real relationship isn't built on lies and deceit. I don't want to ever hurt you like my father hurt my mother. I want you to trust me and respect me, Tina. And I want us to stay together. Not just for a while, but for the rest of our lives.'

She looked at him for what felt like an eternity. And then she did something so wonderful and warm that he almost broke down. She folded him into her arms and told him not to worry, that Bonnie would be all right, that she *did* trust and respect him, and that, yes, she wanted them to stay together too. For the rest of their lives.

CHAPTER EIGHTEEN

TINA sat in the small waiting room, her hands cradled around a polystyrene mug of coffee. Dominic sat across from her, his elbows on his knees, his head buried in his hands. Ida had long been sent home to get some rest.

'We don't want you getting sick too, Mum,' Dominic had told Ida after the three of them had sat up with Bonnie all night. Now it was approaching noon, and Dominic and Tina had finally abandoned Bonnie's room to get something to drink.

'Dominic, stop torturing yourself,' Tina said, though she understood what he was going through.

Or maybe she didn't. She loved Bonnie, but she wasn't the baby's real mother.

Dominic straightened, and Tina was shocked by his appearance. 'I think you should go home too, Dominic,' she said. 'You need some sleep.'

'Good God, no, I couldn't sleep. Not till I know Bonnie's out of the woods.'

Tina was still amazed by the depth and intensity of Dominic's feelings. No one could doubt he loved Bonnie now. No one.

Tina didn't doubt he loved *her*, too. She still could hardly believe what he'd done to win her.

How ironic that the lie he'd told had turned out to be true! Life could be so perverse. After all, who would have believed that *she'd* end up falling in love

173

with the father of Sarah's baby, the man she'd thought she despised.

Though maybe it *wasn't* perverse. Maybe it was written...

Tina was deep in thought when Bonnie's nurse popped a smiling face into the room and said, 'Good news. Bonnie's lungs are much better. Her temperature's down and she's awake, complaining her head off. Would one of you like to come and give her her bottle?'

It was a rush to see who made it to the room first, but Dominic won in a photo finish. Not that Tina minded. It gave her such pleasure to see this big macho man being so emotional and tender with his little daughter. Her heart tripped over when he surreptitiously wiped away some tears from his eyes before cuddling Bonnie to him as though she was the most precious thing in the whole wide world.

He looked up at her and their eyes met. She smiled at him. 'I'll go give your mother a call, will I?' she suggested.

'Would you?'

'Of course.' And while she was at it a trip to the ladies' room was in order by the way she was feeling. Tina shook her head wryly as she walked along the corridor. If there was one thing she could rely on in life, it was the regularity of her cycle.

Which was just as well, she realised. As much as Dominic had finally embraced fatherhood with a passion, Tina didn't think he could handle a further little addition to his life at the moment.

They were driving home from the hospital that evening when Dominic put paid to *that* little theory. He put paid to another belief she'd had about him as well.

'I think we should get married, Tina,' he said out of the blue, and then, without giving her time to blink, he added, 'And I think we should try for a brother or sister for Bonnie straight away.'

Tina sat there, absolutely speechless.

'I realise now what I missed out on where Bonnie is concerned,' he went on in all seriousness. 'I want to experience everything, Tina. I want to be there from the start. I want to be there when my son or daughter is born. I want to help choose the name. I want to be a part of everything next time. And the next. And the next.'

Tina gulped. 'Er...run those 'nexts' by me again? How many were there?'

He smiled over at her. 'Don't go telling me you're afraid. Not my Tina. Why, you're the bravest, strongest, most courageous woman I've ever met. I'll never forget the way you looked at me in the office that first time, and then when I got home that night. I didn't intimidate you one bit, did I?'

Tina smiled. If only he knew...

'Do I have any say in any of this?' she asked, her eyes sparkling at him.

'How about yes, yes and yes?'

'You're rushing me, as usual. First into bed, and now into marriage and babies.'

'It's only called rushing when you're not sure. When you are, it's called decisiveness. So what's it to be, my darling?'

'I can't think straight when you talk dirty to me.'

He grinned. 'Then you agree? Marriage and babies?'

'I might as well. Lord knows what devious methods you'll use to get me to agree if I say no.'

'And you'll throw away that pill you've been taking?'

Tina didn't think it was the right moment to say *What pill?* 'Er...don't you think we should wait till we're married?'

'Hell, no. Knowing my mother, that'll take ages. She'll want all that white dress and church and stuff. I want a baby with you, Tina. And I want it as soon as possible.'

A man of decision, her Dominic.

'Okay,' she agreed, and he grinned.

'That's my girl.'

'I am that, Dominic. And you're my man.'

'For the rest of your life, my darling.'

Her heart filled at the certainty in his voice and the love in his eyes.

'Whatever is your mother going to say?'

'She's going to be so happy she'll be obnoxious.'

'I don't believe it!' Ida exclaimed when she heard the news. 'I mean...you two couldn't stand each other last week. Oh, I see, you're just doing this for Bonnie, is that it?'

Dominic put his arm around Tina. 'Mum,' he said sternly. 'Do you honestly think I would marry for anything other than true love?'

'Well...er...I wouldn't put it past you!' she said defensively.

'I *love* Tina. I've loved her for some time. Tina loves me too, don't you darling?'

'Truly, madly, deeply,' she returned.

Ida was still not looking as happy as they'd thought she would. 'But...where are you going to live?' she asked a little plaintively.

Tina didn't give Dominic a chance to say a word,

jumping in first. 'Right here, Ida,' she said. 'If you'll be kind enough to have us, that is.'

'I think I could just about stand it,' she said, trying to hide her pleasure.

'Yes, but will I?' Dominic muttered under his breath.

Dominic went to work extra early Tuesday morning, because he was taking the afternoon off. Bonnie was being allowed home from hospital and he wanted to be there. He found it hard to put his mind to the present state of the economy, along with the fall in commodity prices, but forced himself. After all, he had added responsibilities now. And more to come. He couldn't wait till Tina's period finished and he could get on with making another baby.

And to think if it hadn't been for a failed condom, he would never have known the wonder of father-hood. Not to mention love. How he had lasted thirty-three years without love, he had no idea!

Tina was a fantastic girl. Fancy her putting aside her acting career just like that to have a family. With-out any coercion on his part, she'd made the decision to become a full-time mother to Bonnie and whatever other children they had.

Not that he'd hold her to it. If she ever wanted to return to the stage, or television, or whatever, he would support her wholeheartedly. A girl as smart and spirited as Tina might need creative outlets outside the home at some time in the future.

Still, he would cross that bridge when they came to it!

Doris interrupted his happy thoughts by bringing in the morning mail. 'A parcel for you, Mr Hunter,' she

said, and popped it on his desk. 'It was marked for
your attention only.'

'Thank you, Doris.'

He frowned at the small book-sized package.

Shrugging, Dominic ripped it open and tipped the
contents out onto the desk.

It wasn't a book. It was a diary. Flowers on the
cover. And fairly new-looking. A letter accompanied
it.

Dear Mr Hunter
You told me to let you know if I remembered any-
thing else Sarah might have told me. I haven't, but
I recently moved into the bedsit Sarah occupied
and found this under the mattress. I think you'll
find it tells you all you need to know about the baby
and its real father.

Yours, Betty Longford

Dominic stared at the diary as though it were a deadly
spider.

Burn it! came the instant thought.

But he knew he couldn't. He had to read it. Had
to find out.

His hands shook as he picked it up and opened the
contents.

Half an hour later, he closed it and just sat there,
numb. Slowly he rose and walked over to the window, staring blankly down at the street below.

He wasn't Bonnie's father.

Dominic dragged in a deep breath, then exhaled.
He couldn't put a name on what he felt. 'Dismay'

didn't describe it. Neither did 'disappointment'. 'Shock' was more like it.

Till fury took over. What in heaven's name had possessed Sarah to pick up some sleazebag at a pub whose name she didn't even know? And then to do it with him in a car without using a condom. The girl must have been mad!

It had happened a week after the night she'd spent with him. She hadn't religiously written in her diary every day, and what she'd written sometimes didn't give the full picture. But there was enough detail to put two and two together.

The diary contained answers to other questions as well.

When she'd found out she was pregnant, Sarah had initially thought Damien was the father, because he'd had sex with her without using a condom sometimes, and the date of her last period had seemed to indicate he was the father. But when she'd gone to him with the news he'd scoffed at her, revealing his sterility and giving her money for an abortion.

At this point Sarah's diary clearly indicated she'd believed the father was this stranger she had picked up. Dominic had been dismissed as the potential father because he'd used protection, although Sarah did say she'd wished he *was* the father. She'd wished she could have fallen in love with someone decent, like him, instead of a creep like Damien.

With no way of tracing the real father, Sarah had set about having her baby alone, too ashamed to contact Tina and tell her the truth. After Bonnie had been born, she'd become depressed and started thinking of Damien again. It did seem she'd really loved the man.

She'd rung Hunter & Associates, only to be told Damien was dead. That was the last entry in the diary.

Dominic did his best to find some good news within that wretched journal, finding some solace in the fact that at least the real father would never come and claim Bonnie.

He would still marry Tina, after which he would adopt Bonnie. She might not be his biological daughter, but she could be his daughter in every other way.

Dominic's depressed mood rallied at this last thought. Yes, that was what he would do!

But what about the diary? Did he show it to Tina, or destroy it? Would knowing he *wasn't* Bonnie's real father affect her feelings for him?

He worried that maybe Tina's love for him was somehow bound up in her deathbed promise to look after her best friend's baby.

Dominic hoped not, but his pragmatic side insisted it was possible. Tina's love for Bonnie *was* incredibly strong. She might do anything to make the child happy, even convince herself she loved the baby's father. Or the man she *believed* was the father...

Tina sensed something was wrong the moment Dominic came home to take her to the hospital, but she waited till she was alone with him before she said anything.

He didn't deny there was a problem, then somewhat reluctantly handed her a small diary, his handsome face looking almost as worried as when Bonnie had been ill.

'It's Sarah's,' he explained while she frowned down at it.

'But Sarah never *kept* a diary!' Tina protested.

'It seems she started one this last year.'

'How…how did you come by it?'

'Remember that weekend when I tried to find Bonnie's real father?'

She nodded, unable to take her eyes off the diary, equally unable to open it, Dominic's tension sparking a crippling tension of her own.

'I went back to Lewisham on the Saturday and questioned that Betty woman, then left my business card with her in case she remembered anything. Anyway, she sent me this in the mail. She found it under Sarah's mattress. Apparently she's since moved in there.'

Tina swallowed. 'Will I…not like what's in here?'

'That depends.'

'On what?'

'On your point of view.'

'What do you mean by that?'

'Just read it, Tina. Then we'll talk.'

So she read it. Alternately, she felt angry with Sarah, then just so terribly, terribly sad.

'Oh, Dominic,' she said at last, her voice cracking. 'You must feel terrible.'

His smile was rueful. 'At least you sound as though you care about what I feel.'

'But of course I care about what you feel. Why on earth would you think I wouldn't?'

'I guess I was worried you might not love me any more once you found out I wasn't Bonnie's father.'

'But Dominic, that's crazy! My love for you happened almost *despite* Bonnie, not *because* of her. I could say the same to you, you know. Maybe your so-called love for me was bound up in your love for Bonnie. Maybe now that you know she's not your daughter, you don't love her any more. Or me, either, for that matter.'

'But that's not true. God, don't say things like that!'

'Then don't *you*! It's demeaning to my love for you.'

'You're right. I'm sorry. I've been going crazy ever since that damned thing came in the mail. Hell, I've never been so devastated, or so disappointed. Not that I don't still love the child. I do! And I've been thinking. This needn't change any of our plans. Not really. I can still be her father, in every way that counts. And I could adopt her after we're married. Is that all right with you?'

Tina's heart flooded with emotion. 'Of course it's all right with me,' she said in choked tones. 'You'll be a wonderful father.'

'I'll certainly do my best.'

'Dominic…have you thought about what you're going to tell your mother?'

'Yes. And it'll have to be the truth. Look what happened this last weekend at the hospital about the penicillin. No…unfortunately, she has to know.'

'She'll still love her too, you know.'

'Yes. But she'll be disappointed. It's only natural.' He sighed. 'Poor Mum. She was so sure.'

'Yes, she was.'

'Oh, well…life stinks sometimes.'

Neither of them said a word for the rest of the trip. Seeing Bonnie so well improved their spirits, and by the time they arrived home Tina was glad to see Dominic had shaken off the worst of his underlying depression. But his eyes were still a little flat.

If only she could think of some way to cheer him up.

She watched the careful way he extracted the baby capsule out of the car and thought to herself that life just wasn't fair. He *deserved* to be Bonnie's father, not some drunken idiot.

When Ida came outside to meet them, all smiles and relief, Dominic darted Tina a meaningful glance, as if to say, Not now. She nodded her agreement, thankful that she'd left Sarah's diary in the glove-box of the car.

Ida scooped the baby capsule out of Dominic's hands, her happy eyes peering down at Bonnie's bright little face before lifting to her son.

'While you were away the doctor rang,' she said, still beaming. 'It seems he contacted the pathology clinic on Monday and gave them a come-hurry, because of Bonnie's sickness. He told them it was a medical emergency and he needed to know if you were the father post-haste. Anyway, the results came back this afternoon.'

'I'll go get them after we've settled Bonnie,' Dominic said tautly, and Tina's heart went out to him. 'But first, Mum, perhaps...'

'You don't have to go get them, silly. The doctor told me over the phone. Can't you tell?' She began shaking her head at her son. 'I do wish I was a betting person, because I could have made a fortune on this if I'd put some bets on earlier!'

Tina forgot to breathe while Dominic simply looked shell-shocked.

Ida began to look exasperated. 'For pity's sake, why are you both standing there like stunned mullets? It's not as if we weren't ninety-nine per cent sure of the result, especially after what Joanna told me. Of course, if you hadn't been so pig-headed, Dominic, I could have shown you on that very first day how many of your genes Bonnie had inherited. She even has the Hunter birthmark! But you men always think you know everything.'

Dominic didn't know whether to kill his mother, or kiss her.

'What birthmark?'

'The one behind her ear? Both you and Mark have one. Your father did too.'

'We do?'

'Yes. Haven't you ever noticed?'

'I can't see behind my ears. And I didn't make a practice of inspecting Mark's.'

'Well, it's there. Trust me. Mothers wash behind little boys' ears a lot.'

Dominic couldn't help it. He started to laugh. His eyes met Tina's, but she wasn't laughing. She was crying. With undisguised happiness.

Ida looked from one to the other in bewilderment. 'Come on, Bonnie dear,' she said, shaking her head at them both. 'Best get you inside out of the sun. Your parents have temporarily gone mad. Anyone would think they'd just been told they'd won the lottery.'

'Better than the lottery, isn't it, my darling?' Dominic said, putting an arm around Tina's shoulders.

'It's a miracle,' she sniffed.

'Yes,' Dominic agreed. 'Yes, it surely is. Which reminds me...'

'What?'

'I was thinking of going to church tomorrow morning. Care to accompany me?'

EPILOGUE

TINA knelt down and arranged the red roses in the built-in vase, thinking how well they always looked against the grey marble grave and headstone.

'Hello, Sarah,' she said as she worked. 'Here I am again to tell you all the news. All good, so not to worry. Bonnie started going to kindergarten a while back. Just two days a week. She didn't want to go at first. Didn't want to leave her precious baby brothers. She's just like you, you know. A born little mother. I was in such a quandary that first morning. When Bonnie started crying, I almost relented and told her she didn't have to go, but Dominic insisted, and of course he was right. Now she loves it.'

The flowers fixed, Tina settled herself more comfortably on the soft grass verge next to Sarah's grave, stretching out and lying on her side.

'I have some special news for you, my friend,' she murmured. 'I'm pregnant again. Just on four months. Dominic's thrilled to pieces. Not too many men would be, what with Stevie not even out of nappies yet, but he just loves being a dad. Lord knows how it happened, though. The pregnancy, that is. I thought breastfeeding was supposed to stop such things. But, as we both know, Dominic could probably get a girl pregnant wearing lead piping.'

Tina laughed softly. 'Not the girl. Dominic, I mean. Actually, that man continues to amaze me in more ways than one. Do you know, we all trot off to church

185

every Sunday? I mean…can you imagine me in church, Sarah?'

Tina rolled her eyes to the heavens, then smiled. 'To be honest, I think it's rather nice. And it's good for the kids. Bonnie loves it, although I'm not sure if it's church she loves or getting dressed up. Chip off the old block there, dear heart. She's going to be a beauty too, just like her mummy. Dominic will have his work cut out for him, keeping the boys away. His mother teases him about it all the time. But he's up to task, believe me. I've never known a man so loving and protective of his daughter. Yet he doesn't spoil her. He's quite firm. But she loves him to death.

'I love him too, Sarah. More than I would ever have thought possible. Certainly more than *you* thought possible. But it's so good to have a partner who knows where he's going in life. We grew up without security, Sarah, and if ever there was a man who exudes security, it's Dominic.

'He exudes a few other wonderful qualities as well,' she whispered, spying her handsome husband walking slowly towards her, looking sexier than ever. No wonder she'd spent most of the last few years pregnant!

Fatherhood certainly suited him. He looked perfectly relaxed and content with ten-month-old Stevie propped on one hip and two-year-old Beau holding his spare hand whilst his three-year-old daughter skipped by his other side. He'd taken them all for a walk so Tina had a chance to talk privately to Sarah, something she liked to do.

'Anyway, my dearest friend,' Tina said, her heart catching. 'I hope you think I'm doing a good job raising Bonnie. I also hope you've finally forgiven me for letting you down the way I did before she was born. You know, I used to wish you'd told me you were pregnant. But now I think maybe there was some higher purpose to everything that happened. Maybe it was written.'

Tina stood up, throwing a warm smile in the direction of her approaching family. 'They're a good-looking bunch, aren't they?' she whispered, her gaze full of pride and love as it roved over the four of them. 'Oh, and one last thing. The ultrasound showed my baby's a girl this time. When I told Dominic he suggested we call her Sarah. I thought it was a lovely idea. I hope you don't mind.'

Tina didn't think she would.

'All those girlie secrets shared yet?' Dominic asked with a teasing smile.

'Pretty well.'

'In that case, it's time to go home. Stevie needs a nappy change and a feed, and Beau has just announced he wants a gog. So I thought after lunch we'd go gog-hunting.'

'Oh, no, not a gog,' Tina groaned.

'Yes, a gog, Mummy!' Beau insisted. 'A *big* gog!'

'Not a *big* one,' she protested.

'Yes, a big one,' Bonnie chimed in.

'And are *you* going to look after it, missie?' Tina asked her.

'Yes,' she pronounced solemnly. 'I promise.'

And so a dog joined the Hunter household, a big black dog named Bill. He wasn't as good-looking as the rest of the inmates, but he was well loved. And well looked after.

Dominic saw to that.

Looking For More Romance?

Visit Romance.net

Look us up on-line at: http://www.romance.net

Check in daily for these and other exciting features:

Hot off the press

View all current titles, and purchase them on-line.

What do the stars have in store for you?

Horoscope

Hot deals

Exclusive offers available only at Romance.net

Plus, don't miss our interactive quizzes, contests and bonus gifts.

PWEB